"To two old friends running into one another."

Addy raised the glass to her lips and took a long sip. "Your mom told you about the divorce?"

"I'm sorry." He reached across and covered her hand with his.

Addy couldn't say anything for a moment. He turned her palm over, squeezed her hand tight, and she held on as if it were a lifeline. Finally she said, "I know what all the marriage manuals say. That when something like this happens, the affair isn't the problem. It's a symptom."

"It still hurts."

"That from personal experience?"

"Yep."

Culley glanced away, a cloud of something that looked like sadness in his eyes. Not what she would have expected of the Culley Rutherford she had known in high school.

Dear Reader,

Every now and then I hear people say reading can't be what it once was. There are too many other forms of media to choose from. While it's true we have many choices these days when it comes to entertainment, I noticed something on a recent trip to a hair salon in Dallas, Texas, that reassured me books are doing just fine.

This was one of those great places where they offer you hot tea and massage your hands while you're getting your hair washed with flaxseed shampoo. It was a Saturday, and the place was busier than a hive of bees. While I waited for my appointment, I noticed how many people were reading. An older lady with a Larry McMurtry, a twentysomething young woman with a Nora Roberts. A mother with a baby in tow snatching paragraphs of something that looked light and fun. A gray-haired man waiting for his wife, deep into James Patterson. And really, it seemed as if they were all enjoying the opportunity to read every bit as much as they were enjoying the salon's exceptionally nice treatment.

I think those people all knew what I know about reading. That even with all the entertainment we have to choose from today, there's something special about a book. Maybe it's the one-on-one connection we have with the characters, or the fact that we can keep turning the pages without commercial interruption. And what a pleasure it is to read the first page and think, "Ah, this is going to be a good story."

That's what I wish for you. Many, many good stories!

All best,

Inglath Cooper

P.S. Please visit my Web site at inglathcooper.com. Write to me at P.O. Box 973, Rocky Mount, VA 24151.

Unfinished Business
Inglath Cooper

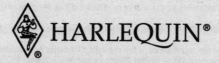

HARLEQUIN®

TORONTO • NEW YORK • LONDON
AMSTERDAM • PARIS • SYDNEY • HAMBURG
STOCKHOLM • ATHENS • TOKYO • MILAN • MADRID
PRAGUE • WARSAW • BUDAPEST • AUCKLAND

ISBN 0-373-71214-6

UNFINISHED BUSINESS

www.eHarlequin.com

Printed in U.S.A.

To Mac for showing me what real love is.
And to Grandpa Holland for the Sunday morning rides.

Books by Inglath Cooper

HARLEQUIN SUPERROMANCE
728—THE LAST GOOD MAN
1174—A WOMAN LIKE ANNIE
1198—JOHN RILEY'S GIRL

Don't miss any of our special offers. Write to us at the
following address for information on our newest releases.

Harlequin Reader Service
U.S.: 3010 Walden Ave., P.O. Box 1325, Buffalo, NY 14269
Canadian: P.O. Box 609, Fort Erie, Ont. L2A 5X3

PROLOGUE

ADDY PIERCE HAD always believed in the power of intuition.

That little voice had a purpose.

Hard to explain, then, why she ignored it this particular day.

She'd worked on the Lawson case until after midnight, setting the alarm for four and leaving Mark asleep when she headed out the door for the office at five.

She had just sat down at her desk with a cup of much needed coffee when she missed the file, remembered she'd left it on the dining-room table. She was to be in court at ten o'clock, but she had enough time to run home and pick it up on the way.

It was then that the little voice had sounded inside her.

Send someone else.

Looking back, this was the detail that continued to play like a CD track stuck on what-if. What if she had sent someone else to get the file? Would they have told her Mark was at home? Or taken pity on her and left her unaware of the fracture in her marriage?

But none of those things had happened.

Addy had been the one to drive to her house. The one to open the front door and notice his suit jacket draped across the back of the living-room couch. The one to hear his voice coming from upstairs. The words not clear from where she stood in the foyer, but distinctly his voice. Followed by a woman's laugh.

The voice inside Addy screamed. *Leave. Turn around and leave.*

But eight years of practicing law had shown her that knowledge, once gained, can rarely be ignored.

Standing there in the foyer of a house that already felt as if it didn't belong to her, a feeling of dread swept through her, weakened her knees, so she put a hand on the wall and stood for a moment, waiting for the room to stop its listing.

Her feet moved of their own volition, the runner on the staircase deadening her footsteps. She followed the hall to the master bedroom, the voices drawing closer.

They'd left the bedroom door open. This

amazed her. That in their own house, their own bed, he hadn't bothered to close the door.

How could he have been so comfortable that he left the door open?

Through that rectangle she watched the husband who was supposed to have been hers rest his cheek on the woman's belly, rounded with child.

Addy swallowed. Went absolutely numb as if someone had flipped a switch and obliterated all feeling inside her.

Mark turned, as if he'd felt her gaze. Shock skidded across his too good-looking face, then froze there.

"Addy. What are you doing here?"

The question hung in the air, ridiculous, considering. The woman scrambled up—as well as a woman in her condition can scramble—and yanked the covers around herself with a well-sculpted arm.

She was so young. She had the kind of skin that made Addy want to run out in search of face creams guaranteed to halt the aging process in its tracks.

What was Mark doing with someone who looked like she should still be in college?

He jerked out of the bed. Addy stared at her naked husband while the woman made no effort to hide the possessiveness in her own assessment of him. Mark reached for a robe where it lay on top of the thick comforter. Addy recognized it as the one she had bought for him at Bloomingdale's for Christmas last year.

A robe. She'd given him a robe.

Was that the cause of this? The fact that their marriage had deteriorated to the point that she couldn't come up with anything more exciting than a robe for a gift?

The room suddenly had no air in it. Her lungs screamed in protest. She was going to be sick. She turned and bolted down the hall.

"Addy! Addy, wait!" Mark called out.

She stumbled down the stairs. *Don't think. Not yet. Get out. Just go.* Her throat had closed up, and her eyes burned with the need to cry. Not in front of him. She would not cry in front of him!

"Addy, please!" He caught her in the foyer, his chest rising and falling with what looked more like agitation than exertion. Her gaze dropped to his ab muscles. A six-pack. Like those guys in the men's fitness magazines. When had he started working out? And he'd lost weight, hadn't he?

She realized then how long it had been since she'd seen him without his clothes on. How long it had been since the two of them had made love.

She felt a wash of mortification for what she now knew to be the reason.

"We need to talk, Addy," he said, a note of uncertainty in his normally confident attorney's voice.

She focused on the navy crest of his robe, the knot in her throat so thick she could barely speak. "Aren't we a little beyond the talking stage?"

"This isn't how I wanted to tell you," he said, compassion edging the admission.

Fury exploded through her. She did not want his pity! Damn him. "How long has this been going on?"

He looked away, then dropped his gaze, guilt etched in every angle of his posture. "I never wanted to hurt you, Addy."

"You knew I wanted children. You weren't ready, you said. How could you? How could you do this?" The words throbbed with pain, and she hated her own inability to keep them neutral.

He stepped toward her, reached out, then dropped his hands to his sides. "Please, Addy, I don't know what to say. This wasn't planned. It just—"

"Don't you dare say it just happened. I can't believe you would do this to us. Who *are* you?"

He blocked the door with one hand. "Wait. Addy! You don't understand—"

"I understand," she said, the details of their marriage clicking into place like the numbers on a vault lock. All those late nights he'd been working, his lack of interest in her and the fact that they hadn't made love in months.

The anger collapsed inside her, and she felt as though her bones might not support her. She walked over to the dining-room table, picked up the file she'd left that morning.

And, without another word between them, she left. Game over. Marriage finished.

CHAPTER ONE

ADDY TAYLOR STOOD at the corner of Fifth Avenue and 48th Street, hand raised for a taxi. Rain pelted her already-a-lost-cause hair, and her lightweight coat drooped beneath the downpour. She glanced at her watch, waved harder as another cab sped past her like a bullet, tossing a wave of muddy water across the toes of the Italian leather pumps she'd stalked for two months at Neiman's until they finally went on sale.

She stepped back from the curb, reached down and pulled off a shoe, emptied it of water, then did the same for the other.

Her flight was due to leave LaGuardia in forty-five minutes. She had been in Manhattan since Monday, taking depositions from the board of directors of a company Owings, Blake was representing in a securities fraud suit. She'd known she was pushing it, allowing so little time to get to the airport, but she'd been close enough to finishing to not have to come back next week.

Fifteen minutes later, a taxi whisked to a stop beside her. She opened the door, shoved her small suitcase and laptop bag across the blue vinyl seat, slid in and closed the door. "LaGuardia, please."

The driver had thick black frame glasses and a scruff of a beard that looked as if his razor had gone dull several days before. He pulled out into traffic, looking in the rearview mirror. "Which airline?"

"U.S. Air."

"What time's your flight?"

"Five-fifteen."

He gave her a pointed look, muttered something about the taxi not having wings, then rammed the accelerator to the floor, tossing her against the back seat.

She looked down at her lap. A drenched mess. She reached inside her purse and pulled out a couple of tissues, attempted to wipe the rain from her face, only to have them dissolve in a sodden lump in her hands. A complete waste of time.

She dropped her head back, pressed a thumb to her throbbing right temple. What she would give for a hot bath and a long soak. The last thing she wanted to do was get on an airplane. *So spend the night.*

The thought beamed up from nowhere, only to be squashed by a wake of practicality. Too expensive. She hadn't planned to stay.

But then why not? What did she have to hurry home for?

Another weekend, and nothing but an empty house that stood as an all too recognizable symbol of her empty life.

April third. First day as an officially no-longer-married woman. Addy hated the sound of it, hated everything about the new tag, its implications of failure and rejection. The realization that like her own mother, she had been left. Half a year had passed since Mark had moved out, and sometimes Addy felt as though she were still standing in the doorway of their bedroom, trying to make sense of the fact that there was another woman in her bed. Six months, and she had not moved beyond that single truth.

Maybe it was finally time she got moving. At the very least, she could indulge herself for the night.

She sat up in the seat. "Wait. I've changed my mind. The Plaza Hotel, please."

Another pointed look through the rearview mirror, this time with compressed lips to complete his disapproval.

A few minutes later, the taxi jarred to a stop outside the 59th Street entrance to the Plaza. A bellman opened Addy's door and took what luggage she had. She paid the driver who managed to complete the transaction with a single huff and an acceleration back into traffic worthy of NASCAR.

Addy went inside and checked in, relieved that there was a room available, astronomically expensive though it was.

The bellhop, an older man with white hair and shoulders hunched from the weight of several decades worth of suitcases, directed her through the hotel's ornate lobby to the elevator and up to her room. Inside, he pointed out the minibar, the safe inside the closet. "May I get you some ice before I go, miss?"

"No. Thank you. I'm fine." She handed him a tip for his help, and with a nod, he left her alone. Under other circumstances, she might have enjoyed the luxurious room. An Oriental rug, two double beds with a mound of pillows propped high, a wall cabinet which housed the TV, fax machine and Internet connection.

Heat crowded the room. She cracked the window, letting in the sounds of the city below, the whine of a trumpet, the clip-clop of horses' hooves on the paved streets.

With methodical movements, she emptied her suitcase. Nothing inside except two wrinkled suits and workout clothes she'd worn to Crunch, the club she'd escaped to each night that week in order to avoid the late dinners she was semi-expected to attend with her client.

On another spur-of-the-moment impulse, she grabbed her purse and headed back out of the hotel. The rain had stopped, so she didn't bother putting up the umbrella the doorman had just handed her. Barney's was a short walk away, and she headed up 59th Street, aware that she could be accused of trying to avoid the pain gnawing at her stomach. And maybe she was. She'd racked up enough billable hours in the past six months to put her in the running for junior-partner status. Work was the distraction she needed. As long as she focused on whatever case was before her, she could avoid looking at the state of disaster currently posing as her personal life.

She crossed over to 60th and headed toward Lexington Avenue. Her cell phone rang. She pulled it out of her purse. "Hello."

"Where are you?" Ellen Wilshire rarely bothered with greetings. As a newly appointed partner in the same firm for which Addy worked, she trimmed minutes from her non-billable schedule just as she trimmed fat from every morsel of food she ate.

"Still in the city. Currently headed toward Barney's."

"You're supposed to be back in D.C."

"I decided to stay the night."

"And I had planned to take you out on the town!"

"Sorry."

"You don't sound it."

There was a smile in Ellen's voice, so Addy didn't bother to deny it. As grateful as she was for her friend's consideration, she wasn't sorry she'd missed the outing. Ellen's idea of cheering her up would be a night spent in some currently hip spot where thirty-somethings with their own set of divorce papers were trying to anesthetize reality with Cosmopolitans. "I'm still in training wheels on the social scene, Ellen. Rusty and not interested."

"Yeah, the unapproachable signs are hard to miss. Poor Teddy's been asking me for detour instructions again."

A young, fast-track attorney at Owings, Blake, Teddy Simpson had made no secret of his interest. He'd been consulting Ellen on a regular basis for tips on getting Addy to go out with him.

But the thought of entering the dating scene again all but gave her hives.

"Let me guess. You're going in search of a little black dress for a night out in the city."

"Actually, that's exactly what I'm doing."

"Whoo-hoo! Is there a man etched into this anywhere?"

"No. I thought I'd fix myself up, get a table in the Oak Bar and spend the evening with a book."

"Excellent social outing," Ellen said with a frown in her voice.

"Practicing for the future."

"When you decide to stop living like a nun."

Addy smiled. Ellen had been on her case for months. Get back out there. Find someone else, and you'll forget all about Mark.

But Addy didn't think it was possible to forget eleven years of marriage, and especially not one that had ended as hers had. If anything, it had run a stake through her heart and anchored her to a single spot of relative safety from which she was reluctant to move.

"Okay, one more night of this solo stuff, and you're mine," Ellen conceded. "You're thirty-three, not eighty-three, and I can't in good conscience stand by and let every social skill you ever had atrophy. Tomorrow night. We'll paint Georgetown red."

"I can hardly wait," Addy said.

"Just finish the book tonight. You won't need it for a while."

The line clicked off with Ellen's usual abruptness.

Addy put the cell phone back in her purse, turned the corner to the front entrance of Barney's. The customers here all looked as though they took their *Vogue* subscriptions seriously. Lots of black, chunky heels, skin that had been exfoliated and moisturized into a blemish-free existence. She took the escalator to the third floor, bought a too-short black dress and a pair of too-high heels to go with it, both of which dealt a near death blow to her AmEx.

On the way back to the hotel, she passed an antique store, caught a glimpse of herself in the wavy glass of an old framed mirror. She stopped, stared for a moment, wondered how she could have thought a new dress and shoes could fix the tear inside her. Allow her to look in the mirror and see a woman capable of getting past her husband's betrayal. The truth? There wasn't a black dress in Manhattan that could get her past that.

Nothing she had believed about herself fit anymore. If her life had once been a puzzle whose pieces had long been put in place, it had all been ripped apart the morning she found Mark in bed with his pregnant lover. Since then, she'd been trying to put those pieces back together, but nothing fit where it had once been. Her vision of herself as a desirable woman, her once-certain career goals.

An older man in a red bow tie stepped to the window, raised an eyebrow in inquiry. She lifted a hand and walked on.

Back in her room, she took a long bath. Up to her neck in bubbles, fatigue hit her in a wave, sent off little alarms along her nerve endings. People weren't supposed to be this tired at thirty-three, were they? This kind of tired was the stop sign at the end of the road for lawyers who'd been practicing for thirty years. The kind that made them start thinking about retirement and second homes in south Florida.

Maybe she just needed a vacation. Some downtime. Owings, Blake expected a lot from its attorneys. Sixty to seventy hours a week was standard unless they had a big case going, and then it was whatever it took to get the job done. Past that, Addy shied from taking apart her own question. Examining the nuts and bolts of it.

At some point in her marriage, she had developed a fairly keen ability to let things she didn't know how to fix merely coast along as they were.

The fact, for example, that somewhere along the way, she and Mark had begun to feel like two roommates sharing the same home. "Morning, honey," on the way out the door to work. "Night," before they went to bed. And very little else in between.

Every marriage had its problems. Hers had certainly been no exception. And yes, she would take full credit for sinking herself so deeply into work these past couple of years that she had ignored the warning signs. Late nights. Saturdays at the office.

But the simple truth was that she had trusted her husband. Had married him thinking he was a man who would take his vows as seriously as she did. And this was the part she couldn't get past. That she could have been so wrong.

When she'd been eight or nine years old, she'd gone on a camping trip with her church youth group. There had been a heavy rain on the first night, and early the next morning she had waded out into the middle of the river that flowed near where they had pitched their tents. The water had risen quickly, covering the rocks she had used as a path coming out. No one else had been up yet, and she stood in the middle of the once placid river, transfixed with fear. She had known that just below the surface were rocks that would lead her back to shore. But some might have already grown too slick. And what if she slipped and fell into the current? Was she strong enough to swim back?

She had finally forced herself to move, found her way to shore before anyone realized she was missing.

In these past six months, she hadn't been able to make herself pick a path back to safety. She just kept standing in the same spot while the water rose around her.

The bath was cool now. She stood, reached for one of the big white towels hanging beside the tub. Maybe she should just order room service and go to bed. She thought of Mark, knowing he wasn't alone tonight, this first night of their divorce. He had started a new life. With another woman and a baby boy, now six weeks old. Addy had been made aware of the birth after running into a mutual friend of theirs in the grocery store, the information imparted with a kind of I-hate-to-tell-you-this-*but* reservation, beneath which was hidden an almost malicious glee to be the first to reveal the news.

One thing was true about divorce. It showed a person who her friends were. And weren't.

Suddenly, Addy was sick of rehashing the same stuff she'd been rehashing for six months. She would put on the new dress and go downstairs. Ellen was right. She was spending way too much time alone with her own thoughts. At least in a room full of people, there was the odd chance of drowning them out.

CHAPTER TWO

THE OAK BAR, the Plaza Hotel's wood-paneled watering hole, had a gracious charm that allowed even out-of-towners to feel welcome. It was the kind of place where people didn't mind double-digit pricing for their highballs. Heavy, dark-wood tables filled the room, surrounded by brown leather chairs, invitingly worn.

In town for a medical conference, Culley Rutherford had agreed to join three of his buddies here in a salute to old times. They were drinking scotch. He was nursing fancy-label bottled water.

"I knew you when that would have been two jiggers of J.D." This from Paul Evans, his old roommate from Hopkins.

"Too much to hope I've matured since then?" Culley asked in a neutral voice while a knife of familiar pain did a slow turn inside him, its edges sharp enough to make him wish he'd never agreed to this buddies-weekend.

"We're supposed to be taking advantage of this, aren't we?" Paul held up the red-embered tip of the thirty-five-dollar cigar he'd been pretending to smoke for the past hour and a half. "We're in New York City, the Oak Bar, no less. No wives. No children. No patients. I've seen at least fifteen bombshells walk through that door since we got here," he said with a meaningful head tilt toward the bar entrance. "Does life get any better?"

Culley had once been the least serious of the foursome. And there had been a time—surely, it hadn't been that long ago?—when he would have agreed and ordered the next round of drinks. Actually, he would have been the one to make the statement in the first place. *Actually,* he would have already left with one of those bombshells Paul had been ogling.

Until he'd run head-on into a wall called consequence, and everything had changed.

Now he was just another guy closing in on thirty-five. He checked his watch to see how much longer he'd have to stick with this group before he could escape to their hotel down the street and the decently comfortable bed waiting for him there without having to cart along more than his share of ridicule for being an old party pooper.

The three other guys at the table—Paul, Wal-

lace Mitchell and Tristan Overfelt—had hounded
him by e-mail until he'd finally agreed to come
this weekend. Culley had nearly backed out at the
last minute—there would have been plenty of excuses that held water—but even he had thought it
might be good for him to try to start being socia-
ble again.

"This next round has your name on it, Culley."
Tristan helped the hovering waiter pass around
the drinks from the tray in his hand, then threw the
check across the table to Culley. He pulled a fifty
out of his wallet and handed that and the bill back
to the waiter who nodded and moved on.

Another hour passed during which they waded
through some of their more memorable med-
school experiences: the day Paul had passed out
when they'd delivered their first baby (he still
swore on his mother's Bible that he'd had a virus;
he was an OBGYN, for heaven's sake, he had a
reputation to uphold). The time Wallace had spent
their rent money on tickets to an AC/DC concert,
and they'd gotten thrown out of their apartment,
spending the rest of the semester living out of their
cars.

And there was the usual guy stuff. Bad dirty
jokes. Boasts from the still-married guys about
how their wives wanted to have sex five nights a

week, none of which any of them believed. Everybody except Culley ordered another cigar, stage-smokers all. They didn't actually like smoking them; they just liked the way they looked pretending to smoke them.

"Now there's one I'd give it all up for."

Culley glanced at Paul who was doing a dead-on imitation of a balding, sex-deprived, turned-loose-for-the-weekend husband who'd just caught a glimpse of what he'd been missing. His tongue was practically hanging out.

A look at the door revealed why.

She was a knockout. Even Culley, disinterested as he was, would admit that. And he'd barely noticed the fifteen women Paul had pointed out before her. With a seven-year-old daughter, dating just wasn't worth the complications it inevitably created. He hadn't been with a woman in—

He didn't want to think about how long that had been.

Wallace and Tristan were busy agreeing with Paul that the breasts were real. The figure-defining black dress certainly gave ample evidence on which to base their conclusions. A low dip at the front of the dress revealed a vee of cleavage. Something inside him stirred, and for the first time in longer than he could remember, he felt the itch of physical need for a woman.

His gaze went to her face. She didn't have the expectant expression of a beautiful woman meeting a date or a husband. There was sadness there, disappointment of some kind.

He had a ridiculous urge to ask her if she was alone.

She followed the maitre d' across the floor, winding through the busy bar past their table.

There was something awfully familiar about her. And then recognition jolted through him. It couldn't be. No way.

Paul, Wallace and Tristan stared like three men who'd spent the last six months at sea. Culley stared, too, but now for a different reason altogether.

Addy.

Addy!

The woman whose breasts he and his friends had been assessing with clinical horniness was Addy Taylor.

Culley got up from the table as if puppet strings pulled him out of the chair one limb at a time.

"You're not going over there, are you?" Paul laughed. "We know you're probably short on goddesses down there in Podunk, Virginia, but this would be ballsy even for the Culley of old."

"I know her," Culley said.

"No way," came back the chorus of three.

"And we thought things had changed. You still get all the hot chicks," Paul grumbled.

Culley tamped his friend down with a look of disapproval. "I'm just going over to say hi to an old friend."

"How do you know her?" Tristan piped up, suspicion drawing his brows together.

"We kind of grew up together. She married a friend of mine from high school."

"Oh, yeah, Mark—" Paul searched for a last name.

"Pierce," Culley finished for him.

"So where is he? If she were mine, I sure wouldn't be turning her loose in the likes of this city."

Culley shook his head. "You always did hold the reins way too tight, Evans. Don't you know that just makes them want to run faster?"

Paul frowned while Tristan and Wallace laughed, their hoots ripened by the Scotch they'd been drinking like Gatorade.

Culley headed across the room on the crest of their still rumbling laughter. Six paces into it, an extended family of butterflies had taken up residence beside the campfire still smoldering in his stomach. How long had it been since he'd seen

Addy? Years. His brain couldn't seem to wrap itself around a number, but he knew it had been shortly after Mark and Addy had gotten married, definitely not since Mark had stopped keeping in touch, quit returning Culley's phone calls.

Just a few feet from her table now, he was struck again by the differences in her. He remembered her in her wedding dress, how perfect and…virginal she had looked that day.

He remembered how envy had nearly eaten a hole in him.

The woman sitting at the table in front of him did not look virginal.

She looked…hot. Paul's word, but appropriate here.

She glanced up then, cutting short his visual assessment.

"Hello, Addy," he said, his voice sounding like it needed to go home and come back after it had gotten some more practice.

The surprise on her face fit every cliché ever used to describe it. "Culley?"

"Small world, huh?" He tried for a smile, but found it had apparently unionized with his voice, and they were both on strike.

"What are you doing here?" she asked, one hand fluttering to her throat.

"Ah, conference, with those guys," he said, hitching a thumb back toward his table. He didn't dare look around; his three friends had lost any nuances of subtle behavior several jiggers ago. "How about you?"

She cleared her throat, looked down, then, "Just here for the night, actually. I've been working in the city this week."

Culley knew about the divorce. His mother had kept him apprised of the details, sparse as they were, despite his reluctance to hear them.

There had been plenty of times over the years when he'd thought about picking up the phone and calling Addy. She'd been his friend first, after all. But her marriage to Mark had shifted the balance of their relationship, redefined it. And then there had been that last, awful scene between Mark and him the night of their wedding. Nothing had been the same after that.

Even after he'd heard about their divorce, it felt as if too much time had passed for him to contact Addy, or maybe he still felt guilty for protecting Mark all those years ago.

"Is someone joining you?" he asked.

"No," she said.

"Mind if I do?"

She met his gaze, held it in silence long enough

to make him wonder if she might turn him down, then said, "I'd like that."

"Let me just go tell these guys," he said, hit with the inexplicable feeling that he was aimed for the edge of a cliff, and his brakes were about to fail.

CHAPTER THREE

HE WAS THE last person in the world Addy had imagined seeing in the Oak Bar of the Plaza Hotel.

She watched him wind his way through the tables to the corner of the smoke filled bar where he'd said his friends were sitting. He looked different, and yet there was a sameness to him that was familiar and somehow comforting.

Culley.

She let the name settle over her, sink into an awareness that had been elbowed out of existence long ago.

They had grown up together, their mothers best friends, both of whom had once nurtured the idea of their children marrying the way some people cultivate prize-winning gardens.

But Addy had recognized early on that she and Culley were different. His bedroom walls had been lined with pictures of a half-dozen stars. Hers had a single picture of Tom Cruise, to whom she had remained faithful until her junior year when Mark started school in Harper's Mill.

To Addy, Culley had been one of those guys who would never settle down, never be happy with one permanent relationship. Girls left their bras in his locker with their phone number written on a strap. She had teased him mercilessly about it, told herself she didn't mind. The two of them had been friends since they were toddlers. And she had her own goals. On the day her father had walked out to make another family for himself, she had decided the man she eventually ended up with would be the kind of man who meant it when he said one and only, forever.

"Hi."

He was back. She didn't miss the interested glances of the two blondes sitting at the table across from them, both of whom looked as though they would have been all for leaving their bra with a room number written inside.

"Hi," Addy said. "Sit down."

He took the chair across from her, and she stole the unobserved moment to notice a few details about him. Short, dark-blond hair. A slash of jaw that, in her opinion, had always been the defining feature of his good looks. He was lean and fit, and she was glad to see that he had taken care of himself. That his need to push life's limits had never taken him over the edge.

He looked up then, caught her staring. Gripped with sudden awkwardness, Addy anchored her hands around the wineglass in front of her and tried for a neutral smile. She didn't need a mirror to know she'd failed.

He signaled a waiter who promptly stepped forward to take their drink order.

"What would you like, Addy?" Culley asked.

She tapped the edge of her glass. "I'm good for now."

"A bottle of water for me, please," he said to the waiter, who nodded and strode off in the direction of the bar.

His departure left behind another gulf of silence over which Culley's gaze found hers, serious, a little intent.

"You look incredible, Addy."

It was not what she'd expected him to say, but she was suddenly glad she'd bought the black dress even though it had no magical powers of transformation. She took a sip of her wine, finding it easier to let the compliment hover, than acknowledge it with a response.

The waiter reappeared with his water. Culley raised his glass and tapped it against the edge of hers. "To two old friends running into one another. A very nice surprise."

She raised the glass to her lips and took a long sip. "Your mom told you about the divorce?"

He nodded. "I'm sorry."

Her smile wavered. "Thanks."

Culley reached across and covered her hand with his. "Are you all right?"

She couldn't say anything, his touch surprising her, then suffusing her with a simultaneous rush of warmth and something way too close to gratitude. He turned her palm over, squeezed her hand tight, and she held on as if it were a lifeline, sure of nothing except that she didn't want him to let go.

He didn't.

He held on while he got up from his chair, and said, "Scoot over."

She slid across the leather seat, and he settled in beside her. "Just when you think you know someone," she said.

"So what happened?"

"Imagine the most boring cliché, and you'll have the picture."

He considered that, then said, "Were you having problems?"

"I didn't think so, but looking back from here,

I guess we were. I know what all the marriage manuals say. That when something like this happens, the affair isn't the problem. It's a symptom."

"Still hurts."

She took another sip of wine. "That from personal experience?"

"Yep."

"So what happened to yours?"

He looked down, but not before she saw the shadow cross his face. "That's a story for another time."

Addy's gaze skittered away from his, settling on the next table over where an older couple had just been seated. In a booming voice, the man told their waiter that he and his wife were celebrating their fortieth wedding anniversary.

Culley glanced at them, a cloud of something that looked like sadness in his eyes. Not what she would have expected of the Culley Rutherford she had known in high school, Mark's opposite, the one whose mission it was to play the field, steer clear of anything remotely hinting at commitment.

Addy pulled her hand from his and said, "Mama told me you took over Dr. Nettles's practice."

"Kind of surprised the whole town, I think."

"No wonder, considering how you egged his car that Halloween."

He smiled. "You know, he forgave me for that, but I think he tacked on a little extra anyway when I bought him out."

Addy laughed. And the sound of it chipped away at a chunk of the ice frozen inside her. Simultaneously set up a small stir of appreciation for the presence of the man sitting next to her.

"Tell me what you've been doing with yourself all these years," he urged now. .

"I graduated from college and woke up one day to find out I'd turned thirty. I think I billed out all the hours in between."

He smiled. "What kind of law are you practicing?"

"Corporate."

"Do you like what you do?"

"The rewards are good," she said, not exactly answering the question.

Which he didn't let her get away with. "But do you enjoy it?"

"It was exciting at first. I've wondered now and then if it's what I want to do the rest of my life." She looked down for a moment, suddenly anxious to turn the conversation away from herself. "So what about you? You have a daughter. Tell me about her."

He nodded, and his face took on an immediate

transformation. "Madeline. She's seven. I'm pretty much a lost cause now. No idea what I'll do when she's sixteen."

Addy smiled. "Some would call that poetic justice."

"For?"

"All the fathers whose daughters went out with you."

He put both hands over his heart, looked wounded. "Was I that bad?"

"Close enough." She smiled. "Madeline lives with you?"

Culley nodded.

"Are you happy in Harper's Mill?"

"It's home. Coming back was one of the best things I've ever done."

The words sent up a flare of longing inside Addy. Over the years, she hadn't let herself think about going back. As far as Mark was concerned, it hadn't been an option. "Does your ex-wife live there, too?"

He shook his head, his expression suddenly blank. "No."

Addy wanted to ask more, but felt his reluctance to discuss it.

"Do you ever miss the orchard?"

"Only every time I get a whiff of apples."

He nodded. "I missed being in a small town. When we were kids, I couldn't wait to move on to somewhere bigger. Bigger had to be better. But then living in Philadelphia, I actually figured at six minutes a day, five days a week for thirty years, I'd be spending about thirty-two days of my life sitting at this one stoplight. Kind of changed my perspective about bigger."

Addy laughed, forgetting for the moment everything but the fact that she was sitting across the table from Culley Rutherford, who, since their sandbox days, had been able to make her laugh.

"So what happened between you and Mark? Why did you two stop keeping in touch?"

Culley looked away. "That was his choice, not mine."

"There must have been a reason."

"If there was, he'll have to be the one to tell you."

"Now you really have me curious."

He met her gaze then. "People change, Addy."

"They certainly do."

Across the room, his buddies were standing, waving for a waiter.

"Let me just tell them to go on without me," Culley said, sliding out of the booth, looking a little relieved by the opportunity to change the suject.

"I don't want to mess up your plans with them."

"You're not messing up anything. And I'm sure they're done for the night, anyway."

She nodded, watching him make his way through the still-crowded bar. He clapped one of the men on the shoulder, laughed at something another said. Gladness washed over her for the fact that she had run into him in this place that was home to neither of them. It was like having a little piece of Harper's Mill handed to her. Comforting. Familiar.

A memory drifted up. A hot August afternoon, the summer before Mark had moved to Harper's Mill. She could still hear the melodic voices of the migrant workers in the orchard beyond the pond. The apples she and Culley had given their horses still fresh on their hands as they'd sat there on the dock, feet dangling in the water, the setting sun warm on their faces.

Addy had been garnering up her courage for days. Ever since they'd gone to the movies together the week before and sat in stilted silence while the couple on the screen settled into one of those mouths-wide-open kisses after which they declare undying love for one another. "Okay," she'd said, "so I want to know what all the fuss is about."

"What fuss?"

"About kissing. I want you to show me."

Culley had leaned back, surprise raising his dark eyebrows. "You need to save that for Mr. Right."

"What if he never comes along?"

"He will. He'll show up one day, and you'll change every thought you ever had just so they'll be like his."

"Will not!"

"Will to."

"Not if his thoughts are anywhere near as chauvinistic as yours."

Culley grinned. "Realistic. Not chauvinistic."

"I'm not like that Pied Piper posse that follows you all over school."

"Jealous?"

"Right."

Silence again, except for the knocking of their heels against the old wooden dock.

"So I'm serious. Kiss me. Just once, and I'll know what the big deal is. Or not."

"If I kiss you, you'll melt into a puddle, and then what will I tell your mama?"

Addy laughed. "How do you drag that ego around with you?"

"It's a chore," he said.

They both laughed then. Somewhere in the middle of it, their gazes snagged, and the laughter faded.

And then as if not giving himself time to reconsider, Culley dipped his head, brushing her lips with his, the tail end of the kiss lingering a moment, then ending as quickly as it had begun.

He planted both hands on the edge of the dock, staring down at the water. "Well?"

Addy lifted a shoulder. "It was okay. I haven't melted yet."

He looked at her, clearly not pleased with the answer. "Okay?"

"Yeah." She rubbed a thumb across her lower lip, giving it consideration. "Pleasant, I suppose."

"Pleasant is a Sunday afternoon drive with your great-aunt Ethel."

Addy giggled.

Culley's eyes had gone serious. He looped a hand around the back of her neck, pulled her to him and kissed her again.

No friendly peck, this one.

He opened his mouth and kissed her like he meant to close the deal.

The intimacy of the kiss shocked Addy, sent waves of never before felt feelings tumbling through her. She made a soft sound and opened her mouth to his, following his lead.

He slid an arm around her waist, gathered her closer. All of a sudden, that was the only thing in the world Addy Taylor wanted. To be closer to Culley Rutherford.

They kissed like they'd done it a hundred times, and it was this that Addy thought about years later. How easy and right those kisses had felt.

Maybe too right, because the intensity of what had happened between them that afternoon had set them both back on their heels.

Culley let her go, quickly, as if not giving himself time to reconsider. They'd never before been awkward with one another, but now they couldn't look each other in the eye. No more joking about whether the kiss had been any good, either. They'd gathered up their things and headed home, both quiet.

They kept their distance from each other for the next few weeks. That kiss had changed the chemistry of their relationship. On the first day of school, the two of them sat in separate seats on the bus. Since kindergarten, they'd sat together, and every kid on their route wanted to know what was up with Addy and Culley.

Addy wished she'd never asked him to kiss her. She wanted her friend back.

She had met Mark on the first day of school that year. He'd transferred to their high school from another county, and Culley's prediction had proved true. Addy fell in love. Oddly enough, he and Culley had become best friends. And just as Culley had said, she'd changed every plan she'd made for the future to synchronize with his, left the hometown she loved only to wake up one day to discover that the reality in which she'd been living wasn't reality at all.

"They're done for the night." Culley was back, sliding onto the leather seat beside her.

"Are you sure I didn't mess up your plans?"

"We'd done about all the male bonding any of us could handle. They're going back to the hotel to call their wives."

She smiled. "I was just thinking about that afternoon when we were fifteen, and I made you kiss me."

He raised an eyebrow. "A real hardship."

The words hung there for a moment, charged the air with something that felt a little dangerous. "That changed everything between us," she said, surprised by her own directness.

He was silent, and then said, "It scared the devil out of me."

"You?"

"Yeah."

"Why?"

"You want honesty?"

She nodded.

"Because after that, I knew we couldn't be the same kind of friends anymore. Looking back, it all seems pretty innocent. But I never forgot that kiss."

She thought about her response for several seconds before admitting, "Neither did I. I told myself every girl is a bit intrigued by the guy who makes it clear his heart isn't up for grabs."

"And I was one of those guys?"

"I'll say."

"Was not."

"Were, too."

"On the basis of?"

"Dating in nearly alphabetical order three-quarters of our class."

"Exaggeration."

"Barely." She felt a flutter of something very much like happiness. Were they flirting with each other?

Culley smiled then, sheepish. "That was sure another lifetime."

"So you've changed?"

"The most boring man you're likely to ever know."

"Your patients are probably eighty percent female."

"Ouch. Another arrow to the heart. Totally unjustified."

Addy gave him a doubtful look, hazy though it was, having been filtered through a second glass of red wine.

Silence hung between them then, while the beginnings of an old connection took hold. They sat there, locked in the moment, while beside them the fortieth-anniversary couple got up and headed for the doorway, arms around one another's waists.

Warning signals blared in Addy's ear. Here she sat shoulder to shoulder in the booth of a seductive hotel bar with an alarmingly attractive man who had once been a very big part of her life.

Time to go, Addy.

She glanced at her watch. "Twelve-thirty. I didn't realize it was so late. I better get going."

He caught the waiter's attention, asked for the bill, wouldn't hear of splitting it. "Come on," he said. "I'll walk you up."

"That's all right, really. I'll be fine."

"Oh, no. I insist. You'll tell your mama about my bad manners, and then I'll have to hear about it from my own mom for weeks."

Addy smiled. "Fair enough, but just to the elevator."

CHAPTER FOUR

ONE OF THE lobby elevators stood empty and waiting. Addy popped on a polite this-was-really-terrific smile. "Thank you," she said. "It was great seeing you."

"I'll see you to your door."

Before she could think of a reasonable-sounding protest, he took her elbow and steered her inside. She pushed the button for her floor, then stood awkwardly to one side, Culley to the other.

The danger alarms were going off again, awareness surrounding them like a force field.

The elevator slid to a stop, and they stepped out. Her room was at the end of the corridor. "You don't have to go all the way," she said, even though something inside her screamed *too late*. "I'll be fine."

"Addy, I'm not going to leave you standing out here in the hallway," he said and took her elbow once again.

To insist otherwise would have been silly—for

heaven's sake, he was just being polite—and she could not deny that his hand on her bare arm made her feel protected and secure, temporary as it was.

At her room, she pulled the key from her black leather clutch. He took it from her, but didn't open the door.

"I'm really glad we got to see each other," she said. "This night ended up very different from what it started out to be."

His blue eyes were steady, intense, some emotion there clearly at war with itself. "For me, too."

The elevator dinged, opening on the floor once more. The married couple from the bar stepped out and headed to the opposite end of the hall, their voices low, hushed, intimate. The key clicked in the door lock, a soft rush of laughter following.

The air in the hallway was suddenly thick. Addy drew in a quick breath, mesmerized by the man standing before her with questions in his eyes. She had no answers. Only knew herself to be spellbound by the moment and a very real desire to invite him into her room.

The thought was shocking in its clarity. She'd been married for eleven years. And she had been a faithful wife. By thought and deed. She'd had colleagues call her old-fashioned because she hadn't bought into their so-what's-the-big-deal-about-an-office-affair outlook, which they pushed like an illegal but socially acceptable substance. Addy's was a live-and-let-live philosophy, but she had never bought into that kind of casual.

Culley reached out, brushed her cheek with the back of his hand, the touch gentle, tender, yet at the same time, tentative, uncertain. "I'd take the hurt away if I could, Addy." He leaned down and kissed her cheek then, just a whisper of contact against her skin. Consolation had been his intent. Of that, she was sure. But the gesture pulled at something inside her, stirred up longings for something very different. Something that might make the awful ache inside her disappear.

"I should go," he said.

"You should," she agreed. Seconds passed while she grappled with the opposing forces of reason and need. Reason lost the struggle. "But I don't want you to."

She slipped a hand up his chest, rested it there with deliberate intent.

"Addy." Her name came out with ragged edges and a reluctance impossible to miss. "You're hurting."

He hadn't moved, and yet she could hear him backing away. He was right. She *was* hurting. Had been hurting for so long now that she was tired of being in this place, wanted very much to feel something different. Was that why she wanted him to kiss her? Did that explain the fact that if he turned around and left her here alone, she felt as if something inside her would break into a thousand pieces?

"Tell me to leave, and I will," he said.

Before them lay two turns in the road, one the end of which she could clearly see: friendship, run-ins every few years. The other road was hidden and nothing could be seen beyond the immediate.

Addy wanted immediate. Nothing more than that. Just here and now. Just this night. Because more than anything she wanted to feel something. To want and be wanted.

"Stay," she said.

An inch of space separated them. She leaned forward and kissed him. She, Addy Taylor, who had no experience in the brazen department, made this first move. She had this awful fear that he might laugh. Think her incompetent. After all, her own husband had strayed. There must be a reason.

But suddenly his arms were around her waist, pulling her to him. And he wasn't laughing. He kissed her back with the kind of quick and urgent depth that lets a woman know a man wants her.

Blind need whirled up, clouding everything except the pinpoint of focus that was the two of them wrapped around one another, into one another.

Addy wound her arms around his neck and pulled him tight against her, not giving herself another chance to consider what they were doing. Where this would lead. To think would be to stop. She didn't want to stop. She only wanted to erase the awful numbness inside her, this feeling of failure without understanding. Replace it with the very real feelings of needing and being needed.

Culley gathered her to him, strong arms encircling her waist, binding her to him. And there in the middle of the Plaza Hotel's fourth-floor hallway, they indulged themselves in the kind of kiss that made all intentions clear.

The gentleness of those first moments fell away under the weight of raw need. And there were some serious forces propelling them along: long ago what-if's and basic lust.

Very basic. And very real.

Culley walked her backwards to the wall. His knees dropped a couple of inches as he leaned up and into her.

Addy forgot to breathe. No longer needed to because he was air.

The elevator dinged again and brought them

back to a short space of reality. Culley slid the key in the lock, pushed the door open and steered her into the room, still kissing her, his foot kicking the door closed.

Darkness engulfed them. From the window Addy had left cracked, traffic sounds echoed up from the street below, horns honking, car doors opening and closing. Her perfume lingered in the air where she had sprayed it earlier.

And with the privacy of the room came another level of intimacy, urgency and haste marking each kiss. She had never known this kind of need, this sense of inevitability, as if the night had been planned long ago, in another lifetime.

The housekeeper had been in to turn down the bed and left the clock radio playing on the nightstand. A DJ's voice crooned, "And for all you night owls, we'll pay a tribute to an old favorite, Frank Sinatra."

There in the darkness, her fingers found the buttons of Culley's shirt, undoing them with fumbling inaccuracy. He jerked the knot of his tie free. She slipped a hand inside his shirt, exploring the smooth, muscular warmth there.

Culley said her name, the sound low and hoarse in his throat.

The song played on around them, something

about flying to the moon, and that was exactly how Addy felt, as if part of her were soaring with this purely potent mixture of want and need.

Culley's hand went to the back of her neck, pulled her closer against him, his mouth seeking hers with a need as quick and bright as the igniting of a match. She drew in an unsteady breath, wrapping her arms around his neck, appreciating with startling awareness the hard, very male imprint of him.

They fell back onto the bed, heads colliding with the mound of pillows beneath the headboard, most of which Culley quickly swept away. Their hands reached for buttons, zippers, yanking, pulling, breaths fast and harsh, as if to stop for the briefest moment would allow reason and logic a chance at protest.

His hands transformed her from a woman whose self-image had hit bottom with the discovery of her husband's infidelity to a woman who at this moment, felt, from the deepest part of her, wanted, desired.

It wasn't only his touch, but the way he touched her. He made her feel as if this was something he had wanted for a very long time. Could that be true?

Maybe it didn't matter. Maybe all that mattered

was the way he lifted her up, up, way above any place she'd ever been before. Too soon, the air got thin, and she thought surely her lungs would burst. At that last moment, Culley kissed her again and said, "Are you sure, Addy?"

She could have changed her mind then and there.

Her choice.

Yes or no.

But for the first time in months, the pain inside her was gone. And all she wanted was to stay here in this place where there wasn't any hurt. So she kissed him again. And he kissed her back.

There in the darkened hotel room, the radio continued on with its salute to Sinatra, and somewhere below the raised window, a horse nickered.

CULLEY AWOKE TO a strip of sunshine that sliced the bed in half. During the first second of wakefulness, a distinct wave of well-being rolled over him. As if he'd been rehydrated after a week without water. Replenished. Renewed.

And then he remembered. He sat up. "Addy?"

He swung out of bed, checked the bathroom only to find it empty. Glanced in the closet. No clothes. No suitcase.

He searched the bed for a note, then gave the desk across the room a similar perusal. He went to the window and stared down at the already congested traffic.

She'd left.

It didn't take a genius to figure out what that meant.

He anchored a hand to the back of his neck. He should have just walked her to her room last night. Left when he'd seen things were getting out of hand. That's what a friend would have done.

But the truth was he hadn't wanted to leave.

The truth was last night had been the first time in longer than he could remember when he had been something of who he used to be. For a few hours, he'd closed the door on his guilt and simply enjoyed being with a woman who had once been his best friend.

In his regular life—the one where he wasn't falling into bed with newly disillusioned women, the one where he was a reliable father of one and a small-town doctor known for taking the time to listen to patients who needed to talk about their problems—he would have paid attention to his own normally demanding voice of reason. It would seem he'd deliberately tuned it out last night.

But it was back this morning with a megaphone to his ear. That, combined with his stinging conscience, lit a flare of urgency inside him.

He would call her. Go see her in D.C. He'd made enough mistakes in his life to know he didn't want this to be another on the list.

MISTAKES, WHY DID they have to feel so obvious? By the time the plane landed in D.C. shortly after ten that morning, Addy's regret had reached fever pitch.

She'd left the hotel room just before six, slipping out without waking him. Every time she started to remember what they'd done last night, she closed her eyes and blanked the thought.

Of all the people in the world, in New York City, why had she met up with Culley last night? A conversation and a couple glasses of wine, and she'd practically jumped him.

Heat torched her cheeks.

She had just wanted to forget for a little while. To find a place where pain couldn't reach her. To stitch back together what felt like a permanent tear in her heart. On that, she had succeeded. For a few hours, anyway. A short-term gain with a long-term price tag.

And now came regret. A big black cloud of it.

If she could just flip the clock back a dozen hours. Just twelve hours. She would have taken the shuttle home last night. Painted Georgetown red with Ellen. Sat at home eating Ben & Jerry's. Anything but what she had done.

Regret, real as it was, didn't change a thing.

At least in leaving before he woke up, she'd saved them both the embarrassment of admitting what they already knew.

It should never have happened.

It would never happen again.

HER NUMBER IN D.C. was unlisted.

Culley had tried Washington information no less than five times, hoping to get a different operator with a different answer.

After leaving Addy's room, he'd gone back to his own hotel, showered and packed, then written a note for his buddies, telling them something had come up, and he had to get home. Coward's way out maybe, but he didn't want to hang around for their question-and-answer session about last night. He knew them. They would be merciless.

At the airport, he pulled out his cell phone and got the number for Addy's firm in D.C. on the off chance that she was already back and had gone there. A receptionist sent him to her voice mail. He left a short message, started to add more, but hung up at the last second. He had no idea what to say.

ADDY WENT STRAIGHT to the office, intent on burying herself under a pile of work.

Of course Ellen was there. Addy walked by her office with a neutral good-morning, heading for her own office two doors down.

"Whoa," Ellen called out.

"Later," Addy called back. She dropped her coat and laptop bag on the leather couch by her door, crossed the floor and collapsed into the chair behind her desk.

Ellen appeared in the doorway, leaned a shoulder against the frame, arms crossed. Her dark hair was pulled back in a ponytail, her face devoid of makeup. She was dressed in workout clothes and Nike running shoes. "Up for a run?"

During the week, the two of them ran together at lunch. Addy shook her head, pressed a finger to the dull thud in her temple. "Not today."

Ellen raised an eyebrow. "So how'd the little black dress turn out?"

"Should have left it on the hanger."

Ellen came in and sat down in the chair across from Addy, looking like a psychiatrist about to get a juicy morsel. "Do tell."

"Nothing to tell."

"I can wait."

"Ellen, really."

"You left the book in the room?"

Addy sighed. "No. But I did run into an old friend from high school."

"And?"

"We sat in the Oak Bar and talked."

"And?"

Addy tipped her head to one side.

Ellen's eyes went wide. "You slept with him!"

Addy covered her face with her hands. "That sounds so—"

"Delicious!"

"Ellen!"

"Well, was it?"

"Ellen. I can't believe I did that. It's so not me."

"It's so exactly what you need. All these months since you and Mark split, and you haven't even been out on a date. Not normal."

"Oh, Ellen," Addy said, making a face, "We grew up in the same hometown. His mom and my mom go to the movies together every Tuesday night. He must think I'm—"

"Human?"

"Easy!"

Ellen laughed. "Now there's one for the fifties dictionary."

"It's not funny."

"Addy, my God, you're entitled. Did you practice safe—"

Addy held up a hand. "Too personal."

Ellen chuckled again. "You were born in the wrong era, Hester."

Addy dropped her head back, stared at the ceiling. "Why did I have to pick him? Why couldn't it have been someone I'd never see again?"

"Because you wouldn't have slept with someone like that. If you picked this old friend, there must have been a reason."

"Temporary loss of faculties?"

Ellen folded her arms, gave her a long look. "Would you give yourself just a bit of a break?"

"Last night…that's not something I would normally ever—"

Ellen held up a hand. "The conscience police are not in the room. Give yourself a little credit, Addy," she said, her voice softening. "You've had a tough go of it. If last night got you away from that for a while, then what's so wrong with that?"

"Plenty, I'm sure."

Ellen got up, went over to the drawer where Addy kept an extra change of running clothes and shoes. She pulled them out, set them on the desk. "Get dressed. We're going for a run. Burn off some of that guilt you're soaking in."

"I don't think that's going to fix it."

"Yeah, but I'm gonna kick your butt on pace this morning. So at least it'll give you something else to think about."

Addy picked up the clothes, headed out the door to the women's bathroom. "Gee, thanks."

Ellen smiled. "What are friends for?"

CHAPTER FIVE

WHEN ADDY GOT HOME Saturday afternoon, there were four messages on the machine from Culley—the first one said he'd gotten her number from her mother.

On Sunday, he left three.

Monday, two.

Tuesday, one.

On Wednesday, his number was on caller ID. No message.

Thursday, nothing.

Addy felt horrible for ignoring them. But what would they say to each other? There was nothing to say. The last thing she wanted was to hear her own regret duplicated in his voice. Better to let it fade. Chalk it up to what it was. A slice of time when their paths had crossed, and they had offered each other temporary comfort. And what else could it be? Spending the night with Culley had not fixed the broken part of her, the part that had once believed in her own ability to choose wisely. That confidence had been shaken to the point that standing in one place felt like the only safe choice. To put a foot in either direction might mean setting off another explosion like the one created by her unfaithful husband. An explosion that would yet again change the landscape of her life so that nothing made any sense at all.

Addy wanted safety.

She didn't call him back.

THE PRACTICE CULLEY had bought from old Dr. Nettles was located in a two-story house on Oak Street in the center of town. It had been built in the 1700s and was believed to have once been an inn that had welcomed such historical names as Daniel Boone.

Culley had loved the place from the first moment he walked its wood floors with the old doctor who had been forced to retire when arthritis made it nearly impossible for him to spend a day on his feet. Coming back to Harper's Mill and starting his own practice had been a new beginning for Culley and Madeline, and for the past three years, he had known a deep and rewarding contentment for the simplicity of their lives. For so long, his life had been anything but simple, and he valued this new peace more than he would ever value any material possession.

But today, things didn't feel simple. Hadn't felt simple since he'd returned from New York on Saturday afternoon.

It was almost six o'clock, and he'd just seen his last patient. The waiting room had been full all day. He hadn't even stopped for lunch. He closed the door to his office, pulled a bottle of Advil from his desk drawer, gulped a couple, then sat down on the sofa opposite his desk, dropped his head back and stared at the ceiling. He reached for the phone, then jerked his hand back as if it might dial the number without his permission. No. He couldn't. The number of messages he'd left had reached embarrassment level a half dozen calls ago.

He ran a hand over his face. Why wouldn't she talk to him? Did she regret what happened between them that much? Apparently so.

And he couldn't stop thinking about her. Hadn't been able to think of anything else since he'd woken up Saturday morning and found her gone. He thought about her while he dictated patient notes. While he read Madeline her bedtime stories. While he lay alone in bed trying to fall asleep. Wondering if he'd ever see her again.

He'd tried to look at the situation objectively. The rational part of his brain told him it was just one of those things. One of those it'll-never-happen-again, once-in-a-lifetime things. Addy had been hurting. She'd needed someone to make her believe in herself again. Fate had just happened to put him in her path.

As for his own excuse, she'd filled some need in him as well that night. Since his divorce, he'd seen a few women. None, seriously. He wasn't interested. He'd tried. But the last couple years of his marriage had been like living in a waking nightmare. No matter what he did, the outcome was the same.

Maybe it was the fact that he and Addy had once known everything there was to know about one another. He trusted that knowledge, had let his guard down.

He pressed two fingers to the bridge of his nose and squeezed his eyes shut, willing the ibuprofen to soften the headache pounding at his temples.

If he had any regrets about that night, they centered around the certainty that the two of them would never get the chance to see if there could have been more.

A knock sounded at the door.

"Come in," he said.

Tracy Whitmire, the receptionist out front, popped in and put his mail on his desk. She had red hair and blue eyes that squinted at him from behind fashionable rectangular-lense glasses. "You going home soon?"

"In a while."

"Better. That little girl of yours needs to see her daddy."

From some, Culley might have taken that as a criticism. But Tracy was a single parent herself, and they had shared a conversation or two on the struggle to spend more time with their child during the week.

"I'm headed that way," he said. "'Night."

"Good night." She closed the door behind her.

Culley picked up the mail, sorting out the junk stuff and tossing it in the trash can next to his desk. Near the bottom of the stack a return address caught his eye. Mecklinburg Women's Correctional Facility.

He dropped the envelope, stared at it for a moment while his stomach did a roller-coaster lurch. He left it there for a minute or more, considered not opening it tonight. But then he wouldn't sleep until he did.

He picked up the envelope, opened it quickly, pulled out the piece of paper and unfolded it. It was the blue-line kind like school kids used, torn out of a spiral binder, the edges curly. The handwriting was Liz's, but it no longer had its characteristic boldness. It was spiderweb thin and shaky, as if her hand had trembled a little as she wrote.

Dear Culley,

I hope this letter finds you and Madeline well. Although I can't exactly say things are good here, I'm in a better place. Have done a lot of thinking, but then what else is there to do?

How is Madeline? She must have grown so much. Does she ever ask about me?

I know I've been given more chances than any person deserves, certainly more than you should ever have given me. But I want to do things right this time. I've been such a disappointment to you and to myself. And I can barely live with the thought of the awful thing I did.

It looks as if I'm going to be released at 80% of my sentence. It's hard to believe I only have a few more months to be here. Is there any way you could come for a visit before then? I'd really like to talk to you. I know it's a lot to ask, and I've asked more of you than I ever had any right to. It would mean so much to me, though.

I'll wait to hear from you.

Liz

Culley sat back in his chair, blew out a heavy sigh and realized he had been holding his breath. There were days when he actually went a stretch of hours without thinking about what had happened three years ago. But most of the time, it loomed in the back of his mind like a dark, dense cloud that cast a permanent shadow.

He glanced at the letter. He wanted to write her back and say he couldn't come.

But then another part of him felt the same thing he'd felt for her in the last years of their marriage. Pity. And guilt for the fact that he hadn't been able to help her.

And with those two emotions battling inside him, he left the letter on his desk and went home to see his daughter.

FOR THE NEXT MONTH, Addy did little more than work and sleep, eating if she happened to think about it. Ellen dragged her out a couple of nights, but the single's scene had about as much appeal to her as an emergency root canal.

She'd actually pulled ahead of Ellen in billable hours this month, the good part being that so much work left hardly any time for mental floggings. Of which she'd given herself plenty.

There had been no more calls from Culley. Which was for the best. And although she felt a bit like a mouse trapped on a wheel, there was enough predictability in her days that she managed to convince herself there was nothing wrong with her life as she was living it.

Predictability was good. But wasn't it always the case that just when you thought you had the tent pegs nailed down nice and secure, an unexpected wind came along and blew the whole thing out of sight?

One Thursday morning in early May, Addy was at her desk when one of the other attorneys buzzed and said there was a call for her on line three. The switchboard didn't open until eight, so they took turns picking it up. She stuck a Post-it note on the page of the deposition she'd been skimming and answered with a quick, "Addy Taylor."

"Addy, this is Oley Guilliams at H.M. Memorial."

Addy sat back in her chair. Mrs. Guilliams had once been her Sunday school teacher. She hadn't heard her name in years. "Yes, Mrs. Guilliams. How are you?"

"I'm fine, dear. I'm so sorry to be calling you with news like this, but your mother was brought into the emergency room a few minutes ago. She asked me to call you."

Addy's stomach dropped. The pen she'd been holding fell from her hand, alarm skittering through her. "What's wrong?"

"We're not sure. We're running some tests now."

She sat for a moment, too stunned to respond.

"Addy?"

"Yes?"

"Are you all right?"

"Yes. I'll be there as quickly as I can."

"All right, dear."

Addy hung up, her hand lingering on the phone. She pictured her mother on the orchard's old red Massey Ferguson tractor, mowing between rows of Red Delicious apple trees. Planting new seedlings in a converted hay field. Her mother had always been the picture of health.

A sudden clutch of fear propelled her into motion. She shoved her laptop into its bag, grabbed her purse and left the office.

SHE GOT A SEAT on a flight to Charlotte, North Carolina. From there, she picked up a connecting commuter flight to Roanoke, Virginia. At the airport, she'd called Ellen and told her where she was going.

The flight was a short one, but there was ample enough time for worry to get a better foothold. Her mother was the strongest woman she'd ever known. Addy couldn't imagine her sick. She wasn't sure she'd ever seen her with anything more than a two-day cold.

Right behind the worry came a surge of remorse for the fact that she hadn't been home in nearly a year. She'd planned a couple of visits, canceled both times at the last minute when something else had come up. And the really terrible thing was that she'd been just the slightest bit relieved.

It was easier not to see her. Easier not to look at the fractures in their relationship. Somehow, talking on the phone, they could pretend everything was normal. Ask about each other's lives, work and friends. Gloss over the awkwardness.

It was awful, but it was true.

In Roanoke, she rented a car to drive the forty-five minutes to Harper's Mill and pulled into the hospital parking lot just after two. It had been built in the sixties, a one-level redbrick building that had recently had a new wing added to it so that the hospital looked more like its modern cousin. Addy parked and jogged across the lot to the main entrance, stopped at the information desk to ask where she could find her mother.

A young woman with round cheeks and a smile that reached her eyes pecked a few keys on the computer and said, "She's been checked into room 115. To your right."

"Thank you," Addy said and hurried down the hall.

Outside the room stood Ida Rutherford, Claire's best friend. Also Culley's mother. Age had rounded Ida's short frame, but as always, she was as neatly dressed as if she'd just come from a meeting at church. Ida was a woman who naturally projected comfort, and Addy was overwhelmingly glad to see her. "Addy, dear," she said, opening her arms.

Addy stepped into her embrace, and a small sob slid from her throat.

"Claire's going to be just fine. Your mama is a strong woman. Don't you forget that," Ida said, patting her shoulder.

Addy stepped back, wiped her eyes with her thumb. "What happened?"

Ida reached in her purse, handed her a tissue. "I'll leave that to Dr. Moore. I hope you don't mind, but I called Culley also, and he's been by twice to check on her."

Addy tried to smile, nodded and said, "Thank you, Ida."

"Go in, sweetie," Ida said, squeezing her hand. "You'll feel better seeing her."

Addy stepped into the room, stopping at the foot of the bed. Another wave of emotion surged up at the sight of her mother.

Against the stark white sheets, she looked tired and vulnerable. Addy had never associated either of those things with her before. To Addy, Claire had always seemed to have stores of extra energy. But strangest of all was to see her with her defenses down. The image she carried of her mother was one of determination and strength. Claire was a woman who took her knocks and kept going. When life got tough, she got tougher.

Claire opened her eyes now, blinked once as if she doubted what she was seeing, then smiled. "Hi, honey."

Addy moved closer, took her mother's hand. "Hi, Mama. What are you doing in here?"

"The cruises were all booked."

Addy tried to smile. "How are you feeling?"

"I'm okay. You didn't need to come all this way."

"Of course I did." She fell silent for a moment,

awkwardness making the words stick in her throat. "I haven't spoken with your doctor yet. But as soon as he—"

"Don't worry. A day or two of rest, and I'll be good as new."

"No doubt about that." The comment came from just outside the room door.

Addy looked up and met the kind-eyed gaze of an older man in a white coat. He walked across the floor, stuck out his hand. "I'm Dr. Moore. You must be the daughter Claire is so proud of."

Addy glanced at her mother and then shook hands with him. "Nice to meet you, Dr. Moore."

"Okay, Claire," he said, sitting down on the stool at the foot of the bed and crossing his arms. "The good news is you're lucky you didn't have a stroke. The bad news is if we don't get your blood pressure under control, you're a prime candidate. I spoke with Dr. Rutherford a few minutes ago. He said you've been on medication for a year now, is that right?"

Addy looked at her mother, tried to hide her surprise. A year?

"Any unusual stresses in your life?" he continued.

Claire glanced down at her hands. "Nothing unusual."

The doctor pinned her with his stare as if he were used to prying confessions out of patients.

"Dr. Rutherford and I have agreed to alter your medication, but we need you to try and adjust some of your other risk factors. That's your apple orchard out on Route 836, isn't it?"

"Yes."

"You're involved full-time then?"

"I am."

"Any way you could cut back some of those hours?"

"Not any way I can see."

The doctor put his clipboard on his knee and ran a hand around the back of his neck. "I don't wish to alarm either of you, but sometimes that's what it takes to make people create necessary changes in their lives. You are at risk for a stroke, Claire. You were lucky this time. And I'd like to see you do what you can to lessen that risk."

"I appreciate your advice, Dr. Moore."

He stood. "We'd like to keep you overnight. Let you go home in the morning. Either of you have any questions?"

"No," Claire said.

Addy shook her head. "Thank you, Doctor."

"I'll check in on you later this evening, Claire."

Once he'd left the room, Addy looked at her mother. "How long has your blood pressure been elevated?"

"A while. I didn't want to worry you with that. It didn't seem like a big deal."

Addy started to argue, but then when was the last time she'd made herself available to her mother for talks of any length? A wave of guilt washed up, and she pressed her lips together.

Claire lay back on her pillow. "Do you mind if I close my eyes for a minute? I think they put a couple of martinis in that IV. I can barely stay awake."

Addy sat down in the chair by the window. "Sleep. I'll be right here. I'm not going anywhere."

CHAPTER SIX

SHE STAYED UNTIL almost seven o'clock. Claire slept most of that time, waking up long enough to apologize for being so out of it and to insist that Addy go home for the night. "There's nothing you can do here. And I'd feel better if you checked on Peabody. He has food, but he'll be wondering where I am."

"I'll be a poor substitute for you."

"He'll warm up to the idea," Claire said with a weak smile. "You know where the key is. Just let yourself in."

"Be back first thing in the morning." She leaned down and kissed her mother's forehead. "Good night."

"Good night, honey."

Addy left the hospital and drove through town, taking highway 220 south until she hit the secondary road that wound its way to Taylor Orchards. She turned off the air conditioner and rolled down the window. The familiar sounds and aromas seeped through her, settled deep. Cows lowing in the pasture off the left side of the road. The smells of spring, green grass and moist earth tinted with a whiff of Bowman's dairy farm drifting through the window.

A half mile or so down the road, she turned left again onto the gravel drive that led up Taylor Mountain. Her heart began beating faster. A wave of pure homesickness washed over her at the sight of the white farmhouse set against its backdrop of mountains. The house had been built at the turn of the last century by Addy's maternal great-grandparents. They had farmed the land, raising corn and other crops. It was her grandparents who had planted the apple trees in the thirties, rows of Red Delicious and Granny Smith, shipping the fruit by train up and down the east coast, and the Taylor name had become a standard in the industry.

She pulled into the driveway now, hit by a clash of memories. Summer days out in the orchard. Her mother ringing the big old bell at the back door every evening to call her in for supper.

She leaned forward on the steering wheel, absorbing. She had once thought that like her mother, the orchard would be her life's work. But

Mark had other places, other things in mind, and she had convinced herself she wanted those things, too.

She got out of the car, found the key under the terra-cotta flowerpot on the porch's first step and let herself in the house. The smells were familiar here, too. The lingering scent of bread from the oven. The lemon furniture polish her mother had used for as long as she could remember.

A meow sounded from the living room, a jump to the hardwood floor, and then Peabody trotted into the foyer. At the sight of Addy, he made an abrupt halt, tail straight up in the air. Black with four white socks, his expression was one of immediate disdain.

"I told her you weren't going to be happy," Addy said, putting down her bag.

The responding meow was cat for you-got-that-right.

"She'll be back soon. I'm just the temporary stand-in."

Peabody gave her a look of pure skepticism, then bounded off in a huff.

Despite the fact that Claire had rescued the cat from a shelter as a kitten, there had no doubt been royal blood somewhere in his lineage. The sun rose and set on Claire, but as for the rest of the world, tolerance was the best he could do.

Addy went into the kitchen. This part of the house had not changed from her childhood, and she was grateful for the fact that here, at least, life had its own comfortable predictability. The old-style silver percolator still sat on the counter beside a wood canister that said Coffee in bold black letters. The floor still squeaked in the same places beneath her feet.

On the round table in the center of the floor sat a coffee cup still half-full and a slice of toast spread with apple butter.

Addy stood staring for several long moments, hit with a very real fear of what it would be like to lose her mother. In a moment of clarity, she realized that she had never thought about it, had just believed on some level that Claire would always be there.

She picked up the dishes, put them in the sink and rinsed them off, the faucet responding in its familiar way, one short gush, then a steady low pressure stream from the spring at the back of the house. Red-and-white-checked gingham curtains flanked the window above the sink that looked out onto Addy's favorite apple tree. How many summer afternoons had her mother stood there peeling potatoes or canning green beans, watching her climb from limb to limb?

Car tires crunched on the gravel outside the house. Addy went to the window in the front hall and looked out. A dark blue Explorer pulled into the driveway.

Culley got out, tall and somber-faced. She anchored her hands to the windowsill, as though she would fall if she didn't hold on to something. She could go upstairs and pretend not to hear him. How childish was that? And wouldn't it only be delaying the inevitable? Sooner or later, she would have to see him, face up to what they had done that night in New York, get past it.

She opened the front door, felt her heart thump hard in her chest. It was difficult to get used to this version of him, Culley as a man, lean and muscled, but with enough of the same qualities that had made girls in high school lose all sense of reserve when he turned his blue-eyed gaze on them.

"Hey," he said.

"Hey."

Silence held them in an awkward grip.

"I just came from the hospital," he said. "Your mom told me you were here."

She nodded. "Was she okay?"

"Doing fine." He hesitated and then blew out a whoosh of air as if forcing himself to relax. "Can we talk a minute, Addy?"

"Sure," she said, stepping back to let him in the house.

"Out here's good," he said, sitting down on the porch's top step.

She came out and sat down a couple of feet away, the space between them deliberate.

He sat with his legs spread apart, elbows on his knees, hands dangling. He turned his head and gave her a direct look. "Did you fire that secretary who sent all my messages to voice-mail heaven?"

She started to speak, then stopped. "Culley—"

"So you actually did get the messages. Okay, let's just go ahead and let the elephant out of the living room. This is awkward as hell."

Her face flushed. She laced her fingers together, unable to look at him. "And then some."

"Addy, look, I'm sorry if—"

"Don't," she said, wincing and holding up a hand to stop him, meeting his gaze now. "You have nothing to be sorry for. Really. You don't."

"I wish you hadn't left that way," he said, his voice low and laced with an intimacy that sent something warm coursing through her.

"I wish I hadn't dragged you into my misery that night. I don't know what I was thinking. My divorce was final that day, and I was in such a—" She broke off there, shook her head. "I'm not going to make excuses. It was unfair to you, and if I could go back and do it over again—"

"Addy. I take full responsibility for what happened between us."

She put an elbow on her knee, rested her forehead on one hand. "Generous as that is of you, I think we both know I put you in an awkward position and—"

"As I recall," he interrupted, "it was a pretty amazing position, and my mouth is perfectly capable of forming the word no."

She looked over at him, her face warm. So much for any illusions of *Sex and the City* sophistication. Had she been Ellen, this would have been one of those conversations where she tossed out some witty banter to the effect that it had been no big deal.

But she wasn't Ellen, and she was way out of her league. If she could erase that night from their history, she would. And not because it hadn't given her a new standard by which to compare her very stale sex life with Mark. It had. But because she didn't see how they could ever be friends again.

And right now that felt like a huge loss.

"While you're casting that net of blame," he went on, "make sure you don't miss me. I had a chance to be a friend to you when you really needed one. That's what I should have been."

"I didn't give you a lot of choice on that," she said.

He looked at her, his blue eyes intent. "There was never a moment when I didn't have a choice. I guess I have to believe something was supposed to come out of that night. The two of us meeting up in New York City? Life isn't that random. Or at least, I don't believe it is."

She looked out at the overgrown yard, at the board fence dividing it from the first lane of apple trees. "I might have once believed that."

"And now?"

"Now I'm not sure."

They were quiet for a while, and then Culley leaned forward, one forearm on each knee. "So why did you leave like that?" he asked.

She glanced at him, the familiarity in his voice bringing back other memories of him. Culley as he'd looked the morning she'd left him sleeping, a single white sheet pulled to his waist, the muscles of his back lean and defined beneath strong shoulders. "I didn't know what to say. It was crazy. We both know that. That's not like me. I—"

"You forget we've known each other a long time," he said when she floundered. "I know what kind of person you are."

"But that night never should have happened."

"Maybe. It's been real hard to regret certain

parts of it." He stood then, took the steps to the stone path that led to the driveway and turned just before he reached the Explorer. "I'll check on Claire in the morning. Good night, Addy."

He backed out of the driveway and headed down the gravel road. Peabody came to the screen door, offered her a disdainful meow, then disappeared again. She sat there on the step until darkness swallowed the twilight, and a full moon rose in the sky.

ADDY FELL INTO BED, exhausted.

She awoke to a ringing phone, propped herself up on one elbow and fumbled for the receiver. The clock on the nightstand showed 2:06 a.m.

Her first thought was her mother. The hospital. Something was wrong. She answered with a breathless hello.

Silence.

"Hello?"

"You and the other complainers in this county need to get out of the way of progress." The voice was low and threatening.

A shiver ran down Addy's arms. She sat up in bed, flicked on the lamp. "Who is this?"

"No one cares about that old orchard. A new interstate is what this county needs. Some good advice? Sell out."

A click sounded in her ear. She stared at the phone for a moment, her heart thudding. A prank call? But why would anyone say such a thing? Had her mother gotten calls like this before?

Addy lay back against the pillows, leaving the lamp on. She heard the voice on the phone again and again. And it was a long time before she finally turned off the light and went to sleep.

THE NEXT MORNING, Addy arrived at the hospital just after nine. She stuck her head inside the door of her mother's room. Claire was sitting up in bed.

"You look like you're feeling better," Addy said, pleased to see it.

"They've given me the green light to go home," Claire said.

"That's great."

"How's Peabody?"

"Missing you. He refused to eat the food I put in his bowl this morning."

Claire shook her head. "Don't be offended. He pretty much runs the house."

Addy sat down on the chair next to the bed. "There was a strange call during the night."

Something that looked like alarm flitted across Claire's face, then quickly vanished. "What was it?"

"Something about selling the orchard, I think. What's going on, Mama?"

Claire sighed, looking suddenly weary. "You know the interstate they've been talking about building for years?"

Addy nodded.

"One of the proposed routes goes right through the orchard."

Addy stared at her mother in disbelief. "What?"

"When it was announced a few weeks ago, a reporter called and asked me some questions about it. I said I had no intention of going anywhere, and since then I've been getting these calls trying to bully me into selling."

Stunned, Addy said, "You're not going to, are you?"

Claire looked at Addy, the lines around her mouth more pronounced. "It's not what I want," she said. "But I don't know, honey. Things aren't like they used to be. We've had a lot of changes in the industry. And George quit last week. So now I'm my only full-time help."

"Why didn't you call me?"

"You have your own life. I figure if I can't make it work on my own, then I'll just have to let it go. It's not as if I haven't been fighting it. I guess I'm just getting old."

"You're not old."

Claire smiled a weak smile and squeezed Addy's hand. "It wouldn't be the worst thing in the world to sell the orchard. Maybe this little scare is what I needed to come to terms with that."

Claire went into the bathroom to dress. Addy sat in the chair by the window, her thoughts in a tangle.

Dr. Moore's warnings yesterday had been serious. If Addy had read him correctly, Claire had been lucky to this point. It sounded as if a stroke could be a very real threat if she didn't make some changes in her life.

Was the stress of trying to keep the orchard going taking its toll on her?

Addy knew her mother worked hard. She'd done so her entire life. She hired seasonal help with one full-time employee. There was an enormous amount of continual work to be done. Trees to be pruned. Crates to be repaired. New trees to be planted. Mowing. Weed-eating. Spraying. The list was endless.

But she could not imagine her mother living anywhere else. Claire had lived and breathed it for so long that to think of her without it was like trying to imagine her without some vital piece of herself. The orchard was part of who she was. She loved it as much as Addy had once resented how much she put into it.

Growing up, Addy had wished her mother would come to classroom parties in crisp dresses with manicured nails like all the other mothers. More often than not, Claire would have a stray piece of straw in her hair and apple stains on the ends of her fingers.

She'd been ten years old the day Claire came to the elementary school to serve as a homeroom mother. It was Halloween, and they'd stayed up late the night before icing sugar cookies they'd made using cutouts Claire had ordered from some mail-order cooking catalog. Ghosts and pumpkins and witches. They'd decorated them with orange and white frosting, using walnuts for the witch's nose and raisins for the eyes.

They'd just popped the last batch in the oven when Addy got up the courage to ask the question simmering inside her. "Could you wear a dress to school tomorrow, Mama?"

Claire pulled the baking mitts from her hands and dropped them on the countertop. "If it's important to you, honey."

"The other mothers do."

Addy recognized the flash of hurt in her mother's eyes, but it was quickly gone. "All right, then. A dress it is."

The party was scheduled to start at two o'clock

the next day. By two-fifteen, Claire still wasn't there. The other homeroom mothers had arrived and laid out their cupcakes and cookies on the cloth-covered table in the back. Cherry Kool-Aid in Dixie cups stood next to paper napkins with pumpkins on them.

When Mrs. English indicated they should start passing out the food, Addy asked if she could be excused to go to the rest room. She slipped out into the hallway and went to the front door of the school. Her mother was just pulling up in the old white farm truck. It backfired and a poof of smoke swirled out of the exhaust.

Addy met Claire halfway down the sidewalk.

"I'm sorry, honey," she said, breathless, balancing the yellow Tupperware container of cookies in the crook of one arm.

Addy glanced at her mother's blue jeans. The knees had oil stains on them.

Claire caught her gaze and said, "The tractor broke down on the south end of the orchard. I didn't have time to change. I was afraid I'd be too late."

Addy looked down at her shoes, disappointment whirling around in her stomach and making her feel sick like the Easter Sunday she'd eaten an entire bag of jelly beans. "I don't think they need any more help. The other mothers are already passing out everything."

She glanced up then and caught the surprise in her mother's eyes.

"Oh," Claire said. "Do you want to take these back in with you?"

"No," Addy said. "There's plenty." She turned around and walked back to the classroom.

They'd never since spoken of that day, but it had stood out in Addy's memory as a turning point. Addy had been ashamed of her mother, and Claire had realized it.

But now, with the memory, came an awful surge of shame directed at herself.

To Addy, the orchard had always taken too much of her mother. Made her into someone different from what Addy had always imagined a mother should be. But now that Claire was ready to give it up, she couldn't imagine such a thing actually coming to pass. Addy knew in her heart that without the place, life would simply ebb out of her mother until one day she would just fade away.

And Addy couldn't let that happen.

CHAPTER SEVEN

ADDY DROVE BACK to D.C. first thing the next morning. Claire had put up a good round of protest against her decision to move back for a while, insisting that she couldn't ask her to do that.

"You didn't ask, Mama. And I want to," Addy had said, sensing that beneath the protests, her mother was relieved.

Ellen, however, clearly thought she'd lost her mind.

"You're what?"

"Taking a leave of absence," Addy repeated.

Addy was sitting in the chair across from Ellen's desk late Monday afternoon. She'd already cleared her decision with the senior partner, and although he would have preferred that she give him an exact date of return, he had been understanding enough of the fact that it depended on her mother's health.

Ellen was less than diplomatic in her disapproval. "Who's going to drag my butt out to run every day?"

"Your vanity will do a fine job," Addy said, smiling.

"True." Ellen tipped her head to one side. "But I'll miss you."

"I'll miss you, too. You can always drive out to Harper's Mill for a visit."

"Any good bars there?"

Addy laughed. "You're hopeless."

CULLEY PULLED INTO Smith's Exxon just after three on Saturday afternoon, wishing he could have delayed the stop, but the gas gauge was already leaning left of empty. He'd promised Madeline they'd spend the afternoon together. But they'd had a couple of last-minute walk-in appointments at the office, and he hadn't been able to leave at noon as he'd planned. Days like this made him far too aware of his shortcomings as a single parent. There just weren't enough hours in the day.

The only good thing about working late was that it kept him from thinking about Addy. His mom had told him she'd left last Sunday. And he'd spent the past few days feeling a loss that had no rational basis.

Johnny Smith limped out of the service station, his blue coveralls spotted with grease, one hand raised in greeting. "Hey, Culley. Fill her up?"

"Yes, sir," he said. Johnny insisted on pumping the gas himself. He'd never been a believer in letting the customer pump his own, and the whole town knew he'd be insulted if they tried. "Staying busy?"

"Busier than I'd like to be." Johnny set the pump on automatic and started cleaning the windshield.

Culley leaned forward on the steering wheel and pointed north of town. "What's all the smoke?"

"Just heard on the scanner there's a fire out at the foot of Taylor Mountain."

Culley frowned. "What about the Taylor place?"

"Not sure how close the fire is to the house."

Culley pulled some cash from his wallet and paid Johnny for the gas. "I think I'll run by and make sure Claire's all right," he said, glancing at his watch, and then picking up his cell phone to call his mother and tell her he'd just be a few minutes longer.

ADDY SAW THE SMOKE as soon as she made the turn off 220 onto the narrow road that wound its way up Taylor Mountain. Panic hit her, and she punched the accelerator of her Volvo sedan, taking the winding curves faster than she should have.

She pulled into the driveway just as Claire came running out of the house, pointing at the mountain.

Addy heard the blare of sirens and glanced back at the road. Three big fire trucks rounded the bend at the bottom of the driveway, heading up toward the orchard, lights blazing.

Addy got out of the car and ran after Claire who was already racing for the farm truck parked nearby.

Claire jumped in the driver's side. Addy yanked open the passenger door and slid in. The truck sputtered and coughed, then finally lumbered to life after Claire frantically pumped the gas and banged the dashboard.

"What happened?" Addy asked.

"I don't know. I just saw the smoke," Claire said, her voice heavy with concern.

They caught up with the fire trucks. The smoke rolled up toward the clouds, thicker now, and through the open truck windows, Addy could hear the cackle of flames as they consumed a stretch of the orchard's oldest trees.

One of the trucks stopped on the closest side of the fire. The other two went on toward the bottom of the mountain, and then split directions.

Claire screeched to a stop, and they both jumped out.

"Is there anything we can do?" Claire called to one of the firefighters, anxiety clear in her voice.

"Not right now, ma'am. We'll do all we can."

"Please hurry," Claire urged, one hand cupping her cheek. "These were our best trees—"

Addy pulled Claire back from the choking smoke. "They'll get it under control."

"But the orchard—"

"I know," Addy whispered, staring at the disintegrating limbs of the old trees. "I know."

CULLEY COULD SMELL the smoke through the crack in his window. At the Taylor Orchards sign, he turned left, throwing dust up the gravel road. A Volvo sedan was parked in Claire's driveway, but the old farm truck wasn't there, so he headed toward the orchard. The smoke was thicker now, and he turned off the fan to keep it from pulling in the choking air.

A quarter of a mile up the hill, he spotted volunteer firefighters spewing water at the raging fire. Culley jumped out of the Explorer and jogged over to the group of people standing back from the flames. Claire stood at the front, arms folded.

"Claire?"

She turned, her eyes drawn, her face too pale. "Hi, Culley."

"Would you like to sit down for a minute?" he asked.

"I'm fine," she said, leaning forward and searching the crowd of faces. "I'm looking for Addy though. She heard something at the edge of the woods over there. She'd just gotten back when we saw the fire."

Addy was back? Before he had time to take stock of his feelings on that, she appeared out of the growing number of onlookers, her blond hair pulled back in a ponytail, her cheeks flushed with color.

At the sight of him, she came to an abrupt stop, brushed her palms against her jeans. "Hi," she said.

"Hey. Claire said you were back."

She nodded. "I'm going to help out around here for a while."

"That's great."

"Yeah." She hitched a thumb in the direction she'd just come from. "I heard a noise near the edge of the trees and thought I saw something. There's so much smoke I figured it would be better to have someone with me before I went in to see what it was."

"What did it sound like?"

"Maybe an animal of some kind. I think it might be hurt."

"I'll go with you," he said, touching a hand to her shoulder.

She took a quick step back. "Thanks."

He dropped his hand to his side as if it had committed some unforgivable wrong. He followed her along the edge of the crowd, hit with knee-weakening gladness that she was here. He determined then and there that they were going to deal with what had happened between them in New York. Deal with it like two adults who had once been friends. And could be so again.

ADDY RETRACED HER steps to the edge of the woods where she'd heard the sound, trying at the same time to ignore the tingle in her shoulder from Culley's touch.

She stomped her way through the crab grass, coughing against the smoke, sweat beading on her forehead and upper lip. She swiped at her face with her sleeve, stopping at the place she'd marked with a pile of sticks. "This is where I heard it."

"Wait here. I'll be right back."

He disappeared into the smoke, and she began

counting. When she reached sixty, and he still hadn't returned, she started to worry. "Culley?"

No answer.

She edged forward along the same path he'd taken. Footsteps cracked against the underbrush, and suddenly he was there, holding something she couldn't yet see.

"Come on," he said, and they stumbled out of the dense smoke, both coughing as they headed across the field.

Once they were far enough from the choking smoke, Culley squatted and placed a small fawn in the grass. "I'm not sure if she's going to make it," he said.

Addy put a hand to her mouth. "She's so small. No sign of the mother?"

"She was dead. The little one was lying beside her."

Addy swallowed hard, tears leaping to her eyes. The fawn's right front hoof appeared badly burned, its fur singed in several places. She bent down and smoothed her hand across the animal's face.

"I can take her over to Doc Nolen's," he said. "But I could use some help in case she revives in the car."

"I'll go with you," Addy said. "Let me just make sure Mama's okay."

A FEW MINUTES LATER they were bumping along the gravel road leading out of the orchard.

Culley handed her a cell phone and said, "Call Doc Nolen and let him know we're coming. Since it's Saturday, I'm sure they've already closed."

"Does he still live in the house by the clinic?"

"He does."

Addy dialed 4-1-1 and got the number, then spoke with a woman who said for them to come to the front door and ring the bell.

She clicked off the cell phone, glanced at the back seat. The fawn was still. Too still. "Do you think she'll be okay?"

"I hope so."

They were silent the remainder of the ten-minute drive to Doc Nolen's clinic, Addy's heart thudding.

Culley pulled into the parking lot and jumped out, opening the back door and easing the deer into his arms. Addy ran to the clinic door and pushed the buzzer.

A dark-haired young woman with friendly eyes stuck her head out. "This way," she said.

Inside, she directed Culley to the closest examining room and helped him ease the small animal onto the table.

Clayton Nolen appeared in the doorway just

then, barely changed since Addy had last seen him. He had a young man's head of hair, thick and wiry, above a broad forehead and intelligent brown eyes.

"Addy Taylor," he said with a smile. "I see you and Culley are still out rescuing things."

"Maybe we can afford to pay you this time," Addy said.

"I don't know. The lemonade stand out front got me some good publicity, as I recall. You two were regular entrepreneurs."

Addy smiled. Growing up, the two of them had appeared at Doc Nolen's door countless times with something that needed fixing. Kittens they'd found in a local Dumpster. A dog that had been hit by a car and left on the side of the road. A baby rabbit Culley's cat had proudly dropped at their feet one summer morning.

"So what have we got here?" Doc asked.

"There's a fire out at the orchard," Culley said. "We found the fawn with the mother. She didn't make it."

Doc Nolen frowned. "How big is the fire?"

"They were getting it under control when we left, but we lost a lot of trees," Addy said.

Doc Nolen opened a cabinet, pulled out a few things. "Your mama okay?"

"Yes," Addy said.

"Good. Fine woman, your mama."

"Thank you," Addy said, wondering at the different note in his voice.

He moved to the table and began examining the deer with gentle fingers. She struggled once to get up, but he spoke softly to her and rubbed her neck until she lay back, clearly too exhausted to fight.

When Doc Nolen was done, he turned and said, "We'll get her front leg fixed up. And she'll need to be bottle fed. I've got some formula you can try if you're willing."

"Sure," Addy said.

"Couple other things. Don't let her socialize with any household pets. She'll need to stay afraid of dogs so she'll be okay when you release her."

"When should that be?"

"They need to be three months old before they're released back into the wild. Looks like she was born early in the season. She might be a month now."

Addy nodded, glanced at Culley. He was looking at her, and they held each other's gaze for a moment, something old and familiar settling between them. Something from before Mark, before they'd grown into adults and their relationship had been reshaped by caution and reserve. He felt it, too. Nothing needed to be said. She simply knew it was true.

"I can fix a place for her in the old hay barn," she said.

Doc nodded. "That ought to be fine."

"We'll forgo the lemonade stand today," Culley said.

Doc Nolen chuckled. "Well, a few things do change then, hmm?"

THE OLD BARN had once been used for cows. A dozen or so years ago, Claire had converted it to a warehouse for storing apple crates and machinery. There were three stalls still intact at the back. While Culley went in search of some straw, Addy opened up the stall in the corner closest to the house.

He returned with a couple of bales, and they spread it out with a pitchfork, then filled a bowl with water and set it by the door. When they were done, Culley said, "I'll go get her. Be right back."

Doc had given the fawn an injection of Xylazine for the ride home, and she was still groggy when Culley placed her on the straw bed a couple of minutes later.

They stood side by side, looking down at the tiny creature. She looked lost in the big stall, and Addy's heart felt as if it were being squeezed in half.

"She should sleep for a while," Culley said.

"Do you think she'll be all right?"

"As I remember, it's not likely you're going to let her give up. Remember that bird we got out of the gutter on your house?"

Addy nodded. "It had made a nest on the roof and fallen down the pipe."

"We had to dig out around the bottom and cut open the drain."

"She flew right out."

"That was a good feeling, wasn't it?" he said, his voice lowering under the weight of something she was reluctant to identify.

"It was," she said, a familiar tug pulling at her. They had a lot of history, most of it old, some of it new. That was the part she was having trouble with. How did they reconcile what they'd been in the past with what they'd done together that one reckless night?

Addy dropped her gaze first. "I'd better go check on Mama."

"I'll drive you back up," he said.

OUTSIDE THE BARN, Claire's old white truck rumbled into the gravel driveway, a cloud of dust following it.

Claire got out, looking weary. "Everything's

under control," she said. "Nothing more we can do up there."

"I'll be glad to go back up and hang around awhile, Claire," Culley said.

"Thank you. No need though. There's still a small crew looking for stray sparks."

Culley nodded, then glanced at Addy. "I'll head home then. Call if you need anything."

"We will," Claire said.

"Good night," Addy said.

"Good night."

He backed up and rolled down the driveway, taillights blinking red.

Addy and Claire stood there until he was out of sight, an unnatural awkwardness settling over them. Two people who should know one another as well as it was possible to know a person, and yet standing there beside her mother, Addy realized the distance between them over the years had not just been physical. She wondered if they would ever breach it.

Claire was visibly drooping, and Addy felt tired to her bones. Their clothes smelled of smoke, and they both had black smudges on their hands and faces. Addy's hair reeked of the sickening odor. "I'll get my things," she said.

"I'll fix us something to eat," Claire said.

Addy headed for her car. Claire to the house.

A half hour later, Addy had brought in most of her stuff and put it in her old room upstairs. Good smells drifted from the kitchen along with the sound of something sizzling in a frying pan, and her stomach rumbled in response.

Claire was at the stove, sautéing potatoes in a cast-iron skillet. The table had been set with two plates, large glasses of iced tea already forming sweat beads.

"Anything I can help with?" Addy asked.

"I've just about got it ready," Claire said. "Have a seat."

Addy pulled out a chair and sat while Claire put the potatoes into a white bowl and set them on the table. She opened the oven door, slid on a cooking mitt and pulled out a pan of rolls.

"This looks great," Addy said.

Claire sat down. "Go ahead and start. You probably haven't eaten all day."

In fact, the last thing she'd had was the yogurt she'd grabbed on the way out the door that morning. Claire had always been a good cook, could throw together a meal in a matter of minutes. It was a skill Addy had never perfected. Mark had preferred eating out. She'd nearly forgotten how good home-cooked food could be.

"What did Doc Nolen say about the deer?" Claire asked.

"He treated her and showed me how to bottle-feed her. He thought she would be okay in the barn."

Claire nodded. "I can check on her during the night if you like."

"I'll go back out in a little while." Addy took another bite of potatoes, then said, "Doc Nolen asked about you."

Claire's expression lifted just enough to make Addy wonder. "Didn't you two know each other in high school?"

Claire nodded. "We went out a time or two."

"What happened?"

She tilted her head. "I met your father. He met Alice. Our paths went in different directions, never crossed again."

"His wife died a few years ago, didn't she?"

"Yes."

"Why don't you ever go out, Mama?"

Claire shrugged. "Dating's for the young. I'm too set in my ways to let anyone else in my life."

"You could go out as friends."

"It's been too long," she said, shaking her head. "Besides, I don't need that."

The words sounded convincing, and it was what

she always said whenever Addy had asked. But sitting here across from her, Addy was struck with the realization that her mother had to get lonely sometimes. Was it the change in her own life that allowed for this insight? If so, how selfish had she been not to have seen it before?

"Are you seeing anyone?" Claire asked.

"No."

Claire put down her fork. "Could I ask what happened between you and Mark?"

Addy kept her eyes on her plate. She had never told her mother about that awful morning when she'd walked in on Mark. Never told her he now had a son. Was it pride that had kept her from doing so or something else? "It just stopped working," she said, the words lame even to her ears.

"I didn't mean to pry," Claire said.

"You're not," Addy offered quickly, feeling as if she should apologize even as the words somehow stuck in her throat. She pushed her plate back and stood. "I think I'll go check on the deer. Leave the dishes, and I'll do them when I get back."

CHAPTER EIGHT

THE LIGHTING IN the old barn was dim at best.

Addy opened the stall door and slipped inside. The deer lay on its side. She lifted her head to look at Addy, then lay back on the straw, eyes open.

Addy sat down and leaned against the wall, knees drawn up to her chest. She'd been unfair to her mother. Knew it in the pit of her stomach where guilt pooled thick and heavy.

Was it intentional, this knack she had for hurting her? For closing her out?

Why hadn't she told her about Mark?

The answer suddenly felt too obvious.

Because that would have made them too much alike. And the one thing she had been determined to be as an adult was different from her mother. The only unifying action she had ever taken in step with her mother was to change her name to Taylor when Claire had taken back her maiden name.

When Addy was twelve, her father had walked

out and moved to Ohio where he started another life with a woman who had four children of her own. With the quiet click of the front door and the sound of his truck rolling down the driveway, he was gone. And he had never come back.

Addy's hurt had eventually festered into anger, and she could not understand what her mother had done to make him leave. Or why she hadn't done something, anything, to bring him back. Addy had pleaded with her to fix things, make everything all right again. But her mother's silence on the subject had stood like a wall between them, and with every passing year that wall had only seemed to widen.

From the other side of the chasm, Addy could see her mother now as she had been unable to see her before. What Addy had once seen as her mother's pride and stubbornness, she now saw in a different light.

Sometimes people just changed. Went another way. Left you behind. She wondered if her mother had maintained her stiff-backed refusal to let Addy see her pain, not out of pride, but out of the sheer will to go on, to not be destroyed by what he had done.

She sat there against the rough board wall, the deer now asleep. Would the very thing that had driven her away from her mother finally bring them back together again?

CULLEY SAT ON the edge of his daughter's bed, closed the cover to *A Simple Gift,* the latest book they were reading. He read her a chapter every night, had been reading to her since she was a tiny baby. It had become their special time together, and he valued it greatly.

He was convinced that the love he felt for his daughter could never be explained with words. As a doctor, he'd had people with children try to tell him how it felt, but until he'd held his newborn daughter in his arms, he had no way of understanding the depth of it, nor its permanence.

Having nearly lost her three years ago, that love had taken on another dimension. And made him desperate to revive the spark that had once defined her.

Madeline lay propped against her pillow, her dark hair the exact same shade as Liz's, shiny from her bath. She'd been quiet all through dinner. "Something wrong, honey?"

She fiddled with the sheet tucked up to her chest, not meeting his eyes when she said, "Mama called today."

Culley sat up straighter, tried to hide his surprise. "What did she say?"

"That she'll be getting out soon."

Hearing such things come out of his seven-year-old daughter's mouth never failed to shock him. There was something altogether unnatural about a child her age using words like women's correctional facility as part of her normal vocabulary.

"Yes," he said.

She looked up and met his eyes, holding his gaze, as if intent on getting the truth from him. "Will you be glad?"

It wasn't a question he could answer with a few words, but one that required side roads of rationalizations and justifications, none of which she needed to hear. So he simply said, "Of course I will."

She caught her bottom lip between small white teeth and said, "Will she live here with us?"

"Your mom and I aren't married anymore, honey."

"I know," she said, sadness in her voice. "But where will she go?"

"I'm not sure, but it's not something for you to worry about. Everything will be all right."

"Do you think she doesn't drink anymore?"

"I don't think she does now, no."

"Will she when she gets out?"

"I hope not."

"Me, too," she said.

Culley leaned over and kissed her forehead. She wrapped her arms around his neck, held on tight for a moment before letting go. "Good night, sweetie," he said.

"'Night, Daddy."

She flipped over on her side and shut her eyes.

Culley went downstairs, feeling as if a wedge of steel had settled in his stomach. Madeline had once been the kind of child that seemed lit up with happiness. As a toddler, she'd had the kind of giggle that he lived to hear. Sheer joy unmarred by awareness of anything other than good in the world. In the past three years, that happiness had all but disappeared, and she never giggled. He would give anything to hear it again.

His mom was in the kitchen, cleaning up after dinner.

"You don't have to do that," he said from the doorway.

She glanced over her shoulder and smiled. "I don't mind."

Ida Rutherford had not faded with age. Her skin had a glow to it not attainable even from the most expensive jars of face cream. That glow had come late in life. Culley's early memories of his mother were of a woman whose natural joy for living had been siphoned away little by little until her face rarely saw the light of a smile.

"Madeline said Liz called today," he said.

Ida turned from the dishwasher where she had been pulling out glasses and placing them in a nearby cabinet. "This morning."

Culley leaned against the kitchen counter, folded his arms tight against the knot of emotion in the center of his chest, even as it began to unravel. "Did you speak with her?"

"No. Madeline answered the phone."

"She'll be getting out next month."

Ida nodded, anchored both hands around the bottom of a glass. "How do you feel about that?"

"I don't know," he said, because he really didn't. "I guess I should be happy for her, but—"

"It's not that simple, is it?"

"No," he said.

He had taken Madeline to visit her mother at the Mecklinburg prison several times. More so in the beginning. Somehow it got harder to see her rather than easier. He felt this in his daughter as well as himself. The Liz behind the glass enclosure was the old Liz. The Liz before the drinking. But there she didn't have a choice. He didn't know what would happen when the decision was hers again.

Ida crossed the floor, patted his shoulder in an awkward gesture of understanding. On this subject, he and his mother were synchronized. They both understood the complications of caring about someone who did not care for themselves, only where the next drink would come from.

"I spoke with Claire earlier," she said. "Shame about the orchard."

Culley nodded.

"She said Addy's back to stay for a while."

"Yeah. Sounds like it."

"That's nice, don't you think?"

"I'm sure she'll be a big help to Claire," he said, keeping the reply neutral.

Ida studied him for a moment, looking for evidence to contradict his apparent lack of interest. He didn't give her any. "I'd better get going," she said.

"Thanks for staying with Madeline today," he said.

"You know I love being with her. I am a bit worried about how Liz's reemergence into her life will affect her."

Culley nodded. "I know. So am I."

He walked her out to her car. She slid inside,

looked up at him through the open door. "Some-how she needs to understand that none of it was her fault," Ida said.

"I'll talk to her again."

She nodded once. "Good night, honey."

"'Night."

He went back in the house, wishing he could snap his fingers and turn his child into the carefree little girl she had once been. But he understood her guilt, had felt the same thing as a boy when he had come to understand the hold alcohol had on his fa-ther.

A lawyer with his own practice, Jake Rutherford had managed a successful enough career during the day. But at night the alcohol took over, and the walls of their house reverberated with his rages. Culley had seen his mother wilt beneath the scald-ing heat of that anger more times than he could count. Growing up, the only thing he had wanted was to make his father see what he had done to their family. If he could see, then maybe he would stop.

But it had not stopped until his father died ten years ago, right after Culley had finished under-graduate school. It was only then that Ida began to stand straight again, like a flower that has found a kinder beam of sunlight.

Like his mother, Madeline was wilting beneath

the harshness of Liz's choices. Somehow, he had to help her see she wasn't responsible.

He went back to the kitchen and made himself a glass of iced tea, heading to his office just off the living room. He had some patients to check in on, calls he had intended to make earlier in the day.

He sat down at his desk with his hand on the phone, his thoughts drifting to Addy.

For the past few years, he'd convinced himself that he was content. Life had not taken the path he'd expected, but he had peace after years of turmoil, and it felt like enough. At least it had.

But seeing Addy again had opened a door. And on the other side of it, he had glimpsed something he'd thought he no longer needed. Ignited somewhere low inside him was a desire for more than he had.

He couldn't define any of it yet. He only knew that it had started with Addy. And that he was glad she was back.

ADDY WENT DOWN to the barn not long after sunrise. The fawn was still lying down, but awake. Addy spoke softly to her, offered her the bottle which she had filled with warm milk. The deer licked at the nipple a few times and then began to suck in earnest.

"You're hungry this morning. That's good."

The deer drank the entire bottle, and encouraged by her appetite, Addy went back to the house to do a few stretches before her run. A brown county sheriff's car rolled up the driveway and came to a stop at the edge of the yard. She straightened from a hamstring stretch and waited while the driver got out and inclined his head at her. "You must be Claire's daughter."

"Yes," she said. "Addy."

"Morning. I'm Sheriff Ramsey." He stuck out his hand. Addy shook it.

The other man stepped forward and did the same. "I'm Captain Obermeier with the fire department."

The screen door flapped open, and Claire came out of the house and down the porch steps. "What is it, Sheriff?"

He nodded at Claire, then said, "The fire yesterday. Looks like it was intentionally set."

Claire stared at them for a moment. "What? How can you be sure?"

"Somebody ran a line of gasoline, then threw a match to it," Captain Obermeier said.

Addy glanced at her mother. "The phone calls you've been getting. Could they have anything to do with this?"

Sheriff Ramsey laserbeamed a look at Claire. "What calls?"

"They're not anything I've taken seriously. Just someone who thinks I shouldn't voice my opinion on the route of the new interstate."

"Well, that's a place to start. We'll check out the call records with the phone company. Right now, we're going back up to take another look around. Make sure we didn't miss anything yesterday."

Claire nodded.

"Thank you," Addy said.

Both men offered a "Yes, ma'am," before getting in the car and heading up to the fire site.

Addy stood silent for a few moments, processing what she'd just heard. Claire sat down on the bottom porch step, dropped her forehead onto one hand.

"They'll find who did it," Addy said.

"I'm not sure it really matters."

"What do you mean? Of course it does."

"I don't know," Claire said, setting her gaze on the driveway. "The last few years, it's been one thing after another. First we had the problem with Alar. After we stopped using it, the trees at the north end of the orchard wouldn't grow. We had to cut every one of them down. And, of course, that cut back on our production. We had a freeze a couple springs ago that really hurt the next year's crop. And the temporary labor costs have gotten so exorbitant, it's hard to make ends meet. At some point, you have to start wondering if the good Lord is trying to tell you something."

Addy had never heard this kind of resignation in her mother's voice. For as long as she could remember, her mother had gone at the task of running the orchard with bulldozer determination. "Every business has its rough spots."

"True," Claire said, trying to smile. "But when there's more rough than smooth…"

"I've never known you to give up on anything."

"There's something to be said for going out gracefully. Anyway, I'm keeping you from your run," Claire said, standing.

Running had become Addy's way of burning off the hard stuff, stress, worries. But to do so now felt as if it would be about her needs and hers only. She glanced at her mother and said, "Come with me."

Claire shook her head, looking surprised. "I couldn't run five feet."

"We'll walk," Addy said. "Start at the beginning."

Claire met her gaze, and something nice passed between them. She nodded once, then stood, and they headed down the gravel road, the morning sun warm on their shoulders.

SORE ANKLE, his foot.

Harold Carter had succumbed last spring to a

massive heart attack, after decades of fried chicken and its accoutrements—mashed potatoes, gravy and hot buttered biscuits.

Since then, his young widow, Mae, had been in Culley's office no less than eight times. This Monday morning marking another visit during which Culley had yet to find anything wrong with her.

She leaned back on the examining table with one knee propped up while her other leg extended in a graceful ballerina point. Mae was attractive, some would have said beautiful. She had the well-kept look of a woman who spent most of her time at the task.

He lifted her delicate ankle, gently probed the area where she had complained of pain. Mae didn't flinch. "There's no swelling," he said. "You say you turned it?"

"Yesterday. I don't know how I could be so clumsy. It isn't like me."

Culley rotated her ankle in one direction, then the other. She winced.

"Sore there?" he asked.

"A little."

He released her foot, skeptical, but giving her the benefit of the doubt. "You can take ibuprofen every four hours. Normal dosage. If it's not better in a couple of days, give me a call."

Mae sat up, the V-neck of her peach-colored silk blouse slipping far enough to one side to reveal a glimpse of ivory lace. "Nothing fractured then?"

He shook his head. "No."

"Oh, good, I'm so relieved. I had visions of having to wear one of those awful brown lace-up shoes."

Culley stepped back and entered a few things in the computer on the edge of the counter. "I don't think you'll need to worry about that."

Mae straightened her blouse and then gave him a direct look. "Would you like to go out to dinner?"

She shot straight; he'd give her that. "I don't think it's a good idea," he said. "Doctor-patient."

"It's not a problem for me."

He managed a half laugh. "I'm flattered, Mae, but I'm not looking for that right now."

She slid to the edge of the table, dropped to the floor, walked right up to him and stopped with an inch of space between them. "Look, Culley, we're grown-ups. This isn't high school. I don't need roses and promises. But I would like to have a man in my bed. I'd like for that man to be you. Simple as that."

Maybe he should have been interested. Flattered, at the least. He'd been single for three years. To date, only one woman had made him start to think he might be missing out. "Wrong man, wrong time."

She touched a finger to his shirt, trailed the row of buttons, stopping at his belt buckle. "Offer stands," she said. "All you have to do is call."

She picked up her purse then and left the room.

CHAPTER NINE

ADDY DROVE INTO town that afternoon to pick up a few things at Simpson's Rexall.

She parallel parked out front and stepped through the door on a rush of fond remembrance for the place. The ice-cream counter still ran the length of the righthand side of the store. One wall was dedicated to paperback novels and comic books. Another held a vast display of old-fashioned candy, peppermint sticks, Mallo Cups, fireballs.

As soon as they were old enough to ride their bikes into town, she and Culley had been daily customers. They collected Coke bottles from the side of the road on the way to finance the banana split they would divide between the two of them, eating it outside on the sidewalk, ice cream dripping in big circles onto the concrete.

Doris Simpson was sweeping behind the register. "Hello, Mrs. Simpson," Addy said.

The woman looked up, recognition lighting her face. "Addy. My goodness, how nice to see you."

"How are you?"

"Same as ever," she answered with a genuine smile. "I'd heard you were up at your mama's house. You haven't changed a bit."

Addy smiled. "My mirror says differently."

Doris Simpson laughed. "Then you need a new mirror, honey. Go on and look around. If I can help you with anything, let me know."

"Thank you." Addy reached for a basket and started down an aisle, picking up a bottle of shampoo, nail-polish remover, astringent. She was looking for toothpaste when voices from the next aisle drifted over.

"Culley Rutherford doesn't strike me as your type anyway, Mae."

"Oh, really? What type is that?"

"The player type. Does he even date?"

"If he doesn't, he'd have good reason, with an ex in prison."

"Maybe he's waiting for her."

"Maybe so. But he's got some time to kill. And she who persists—"

"Irritates," the other woman answered.

"Gets what she wants," the Mae woman disagreed. "He's interested. It's just taking a little more persuasion than I would have guessed."

Culley's ex-wife was in prison? Addy stood for a moment, stunned. Prison?

She grabbed a box of toothpaste from the shelf, dropped it. She scooped it up from the floor and headed for the register, too rattled to remember anything else she'd come in for.

CLAIRE WAS GONE all afternoon, forcing Addy to wait until she returned to ask the questions hammering inside her. She was on her way to the barn that evening to give the deer its bottle when Claire pulled into the driveway and got out of the car.

"How was your meeting?" Addy asked.

"Too many queen bees and not enough worker bees," she said. "The church would get a lot more out of us if people would just pick a job and not have to talk about it so long."

Addy smiled. "I was just going to the barn. Walk down with me?"

"Sure," Claire said.

Inside the stall, Addy knelt down and held out the bottle. By now, the deer reached for it eagerly. "I overheard a conversation in town today about Culley's ex-wife."

"Ah. I hadn't said anything because I thought it was his place. And I still think that."

"Some woman named Mae was talking about him."

"Mae Carter. She's a piece of work, that one. I imagine she'd like to get her hooks in him."

"So I gathered."

A car pulled up outside, the motor shutting off.

"I'll see who it is," Claire said, letting herself out of the stall.

Addy rubbed the deer's soft neck. Voices mingled outside the barn, but one immediately stood out. Culley. Her stomach took a nosedive. All afternoon, she'd thought about the conversation she'd overheard in the drugstore, told herself it was none of her business. He was a single man in a small town. Of course, there were women interested in him. Women had always been interested in him. But why hadn't he told her about Liz?

The outside door to the barn swung open. Footsteps, and then Culley stood outside the stall, a small, dark-haired girl clutching his hand.

"Hi," Addy said.

"Hi. Your mom sent us in. She went back to the house to put something in the oven. Addy, this is my daughter Madeline."

Addy stood, brushed her hands on her jeans. "Hi, Madeline. I'm Addy."

"Hi," the little girl said, her voice soft and shy. She looked at the deer and said, "She's so small."

"I was just getting ready to give her a bottle. Would you like to do it?"

Madeline's brown eyes lit up. "Really?"

"Sure." Addy picked up the bottle, then knelt beside the girl, showing her how to hold it.

After a few moments, Addy stood and let Madeline do it herself.

"So she's on the mend," Culley said.

Addy nodded. "I'm still changing her bandage twice a day, but the burn is healing nicely. I think she's going to be all right."

"That's great."

Awkwardness settled over them, and they stood silent for a while, watching Madeline feed the fawn.

Culley touched a hand to Addy's elbow. "Could we talk outside for a minute?"

She looked over at him, surprised. "Sure."

"Be right outside, honey," Culley said to Madeline.

"Okay, Daddy."

The air had cooled, the sun sinking fast. A pair of meadowlarks chirped from the top rail of the board fence by the barn. At the house, Peabody sat on the porch step staring at them with squinty-eyed suspicion.

Culley leaned against the Explorer and folded his arms across his chest. "Is this how it's going to be?"

She forced herself to meet his gaze. "What?"

"Us. This stiffness. Like we don't know what to say to each other."

She lifted her shoulders. "I don't know what to say."

"Okay. How about we just start over? Forget what happened in New York. We can't change it, but we can get past it."

"Can we?"

"If we want to."

"I'd like for us to be friends again. Like it used to be."

"Like it used to be."

She nodded.

"That means no sex," he said, deadpan.

Her smile was instant, surprised. "We never had sex back then."

"What were we thinking?"

His eyes warmed with the words, and she blinked back a sudden hit of remembered intimacies that were getting increasingly difficult to keep tucked inside their designated don't-go-there box.

"Okay," he said. "Friends."

"Friends."

The front porch screen door squeaked open. "Addy?" Claire's voice rang out. "I'll have dinner ready in a jiffy. Just some beans and corn bread I made earlier. Culley, you and Madeline join us. I insist."

Culley glanced at Addy. "That okay?"

"You ate dinner here nearly as much as I did until—"

"You and Mark started dating."

"Yeah." The name was like a douse of cold water. Addy bit her lip.

Madeline came out of the barn. "She's asleep."

"Then you must have done a good job of feeding her," Addy said.

Madeline's smile was shy but pleased.

"We've been invited to stay for supper. That sound good?"

Madeline nodded.

They walked back to the house with Madeline in the middle. Claire sent them all to wash their hands, then directed them to the round table in the center of the kitchen. A steaming pot of beans sat on a hot plate next to warm, buttered corn bread. She poured frosty glasses of iced tea for the adults, milk for Madeline.

Claire said the blessing, and everyone started eating.

The cat pranced into the kitchen, sat down next to Claire's chair and began cleaning his right paw with the kind of care that spoke of a high sense of self-worth.

"What's his name?" Madeline asked.

"Peabody," Claire said.

"Have you had him a long time?"

"Long enough for him to decide who's the rightful head of the household."

"Daddy said I could have a dog if I want," Madeline said.

"Or a cat," Culley said. "So far you haven't taken me up on either one."

"I had a dog when I was a little girl," Addy said.

"Oatey," Culley said. "He followed you everywhere."

"Why Oatey?" Madeline asked quietly.

"He was the color of oatmeal," Addy said. "With curly hair and the sweetest face. Your dad and I found him on the side of the road one day when we were out riding our bikes."

"He was just sitting there waiting as if he'd known all along we were coming," Culley said.

Madeline's smile was wistful.

"I loved having a dog when I was growing up," Addy said.

"I've always been surprised that you haven't had one since," Claire said.

Addy tipped her head, looked down at her plate. "Mark was never a dog person."

The conversation changed direction then, the food disappearing quickly. When they were done, Culley said, "You're a fine cook, Claire."

Claire's smile was appreciative. "Thank you. How about some coffee?"

"If you're making it."

"Already did." She filled two cups, handed one to Culley, one to Addy. "I've been chosen to make candied apples for the church bake sale. All right if I enlist Madeline's help?"

Madeline sent Culley a hopeful look.

"Sure," he said.

"Then you two take your coffee out on the porch and catch up."

Addy and Culley went outside. Darkness had settled, the air pleasantly cool. They stood in stilted silence.

"She's embarrassingly transparent," Addy said.

"She and my mom must have a master plan. She slips your name into the conversation just often enough to be obvious."

Addy smiled.

They sat in the old porch swing, he on one side, she on the other.

"The squeaks are the same," Culley said, pushing off.

She turned her head. He was looking at her, something distinctly nonplatonic in his eyes.

She dropped her gaze first.

"Chicken," he said.

"You agreed. Friends."

His sigh indicated heavy regret.

Which was altogether too appealing. She rubbed a thumb around the rim of her white mug and said, "So you're a hot ticket with the ladies in town."

"Oh yeah, I'm big with the Tuesday seniors club. I have a standing invite to their Hardee's Biscuit and Bingo."

A laugh bubbled up out of Addy.

He smiled.

Addy sobered. "You're big with one Mae Carter, too."

He dropped his head back against the swing, made a groaning noise. "Her insurance company actually called my office the other day to question the number of visits she's made in the past three months."

Addy laughed again. "She may have to start financing her co-pay out of pocket then?"

"Looks that way." His voice was low and exasperated.

She darted a glance at him, liking the fact that they could still tease each other. They'd been fourteen or so when the girls had first started flocking to him like bees to clover. At his request, she'd run interference for him countless times.

"Poor Culley," she said now. "Still beating them off with a stick."

He turned, angled a knee in the center of the swing, so that it brushed the bare skin of her leg beneath her jean shorts.

"There's a Merchant's dinner tomorrow night in town. How about going with me?"

"Let me guess. Mae's going to be there."

"Afraid so."

"Do I need to wear my shoulder pads?"

"One good tackle should do the trick."

"You just need to wear a bag over your head. That would fix the problem."

His laugh was low and rumbling. "No danger in a man getting overconfident with you."

"I just acknowledged that you're good-looking."

"Is that what that was?" he asked, teasing.

"If I get any more direct than that, we won't be able to find a bag big enough for your head."

He rubbed a thumb across her shoulder.

Her response was immediate. She blinked once. "Not fair."

"What?"

"You're off the friends thing again."

"Oh, that."

"That."

He pulled his hand away, stuck it under his thigh, as if he didn't trust it. "So, tomorrow night?"

She should have said no. Clearly. Common sense and every shred of self-protective armor she could muster insisted as much. "Not a date, right?"

He held up a hand. Scout's honor. "Nope. Just friends."

"Okay," she said. "One defensive end hired."

CHAPTER TEN

SHE HAD INSISTED on taking her own car.

Culley had offered to pick her up, but she made a half-credible excuse of errands to run in town before meeting him. He had accepted her explanation with a notable degree of amusement in his voice. As if he were on to her. Which it seemed that he was.

She wasn't fooling him.

Just sitting there on the porch swing with Culley last night had triggered her flight instinct, and she had put her hand on the phone a half dozen times throughout the day to back out.

Eleven years. That was the part she kept coming back to. Couldn't seem to get past. She had spent eleven years of her life with a man she had thought she knew. Trusted. Eleven years, only to open her eyes one day and find that nothing was as she had thought it to be. She felt as if the light switch had been flipped, plunging her into total

darkness so that nothing about her life was remotely recognizable. Not even her own feelings.
It seemed to her that she had two choices. Stand
completely still in the middle of all that darkness.
Or grope around, trying to feel her way.

Where Culley was concerned, standing still
seemed like the safe choice.

She parallel parked in front of the town municipal building. Culley pulled in behind her.

She got out, stood for a moment while he
walked toward her, smiling.

The sight of him was like a sucker punch to the
stomach. Dressed in a jacket and white shirt, khaki
pants and loafers, he looked as if he'd come straight
from work. His dark blond hair had a slight wave
to it, and his smile was of the knee-weakening va-
riety. In all fairness, it should have been registered.

"Hey," he said.

"Hi."

"You look great."

"Thanks," she said.

"Well, should we head in?"

"Sure."

They walked side by side up the brick walkway
to the municipal building. Not far from the entrance, voices drifted out, mingling with laughter.

Inside, rows of tables had been set up with folding metal chairs. At the front of the room was a buffet spread, steam spiraling up from the big silver containers holding the food.

People stood in clusters of three and four, several raising their hands at Culley and then settling surprised looks on Addy.

He took her elbow, steered her toward a group of three, two men and a woman. He introduced them as doctors at the hospital, and they each shook her hand with inquiring gazes.

They mingled for a while; Addy ended up knowing many of the people there, most of whom commented on how nice it was to see her with Culley.

Except for one.

Addy saw her coming from the other side of the room. Like a shark, her approach was smooth and easy, but you could see the fin, knew there was about to be trouble.

Culley must have spotted her at the same time because he took a step closer and put his hand on Addy's back.

"Culley," Mae said. "You did make it, after all."

"Hello, Mae. How's the ankle?"

"Much better." She smiled up at him, deliberately, it seemed, not looking at Addy.

"This is Addy Taylor," Culley said, his hand moving up her back to settle on her shoulder.

"Hello," Mae said.

"Hello."

Mae tipped her head. "Have we met before?"

"No," Addy said.

"Addy and I grew up together."

"Oh." Long pause. "How sweet."

"Actually, we weren't very sweet," Addy said.

"We got in a good bit of trouble together," Culley added, the steamy look he set on her emphasizing the double meaning behind the admission.

Addy ran a hand under the back of her hair, the room suddenly a little warm.

"That's funny. You don't look like the trouble type," Mae said, her smile just the slightest bit forced.

"That's funny." Addy returned the smile. "You do."

Mae blinked. The ensuing stretch of silence lingered like a standoff. As a lawyer, Addy had long ago learned the value of keeping quiet. The first to speak was usually the loser.

"Well," Mae said, stepping back. "So very nice to meet you, Addy."

"You, too," she said.

Mae nodded at Culley, then sailed off toward a group of men, all of whom looked openly pleased to see her.

"Claws on my kitten," Culley said, smiling.

"I have no idea where that came from."

His smile widened.

"That was my last game," she said. "The next time you need someone to run interference, buy a new stick."

The smile became a grin. "Admit you kind of enjoyed that."

"Not."

Someone tapped a spoon on a glass and announced it was time to eat. They stood in line and filled their plates, Mae ahead of them between two older men whose expressions resembled those of big-ticket lottery winners.

The dinner lasted an hour and a half or so. People began trickling out of the building around nine, and when Culley suggested they leave, Addy was more than ready to go. As the evening had progressed, she'd felt the increasingly curious stares from people around them, knew that by tomorrow the town grapevine would have declared them an item.

They walked outside, stopping beside Addy's Volvo. "Bad idea, that."

He leaned against the car. "Why?"

"Because now everyone in town thinks we're dating."

"And that would be horrible because—"

"We're not."

"It wouldn't have to be a lie."

"Culley—"

"I know. I know. Friends."

He looked down at her, something too appealing in his blue gaze. "Can a friend buy you an ice cream at Meyers's? Payback for running defense."

This would have been an obvious place to end the evening, steer it back onto safer tracks. But it was only ice cream, after all. Maybe she was being too much of a turtle, afraid to even peek out of her shell. "They still make their own waffle cones?"

"Afraid so."

"Sold."

Meyers's was a couple blocks away. They headed down the sidewalk, making small talk about the dinner, the mayor's speech halfway through the evening, during which he thanked the businesses for their role in making Harper's Mill an attractive place to live. It was his belief that without them people would have to move elsewhere, and he wanted to make sure the town did everything it could to help facilitate their success.

Meyers's Ice Cream was one of those places to go if you had an urge to send your triglycerides into the stratosphere. They stood in front of the counter, debating over an array of mouthwatering concoctions guaranteed to sabotage a diet. "You're a doctor," Addy said. "You should know better."

"Live a little."

Addy conceded and ordered a double scoop of Chocolate-Cashew-Crunch. Culley got plain vanilla.

"Vanilla?" Addy asked on the way out the door.

"Hard to beat the standard stuff when it's done right."

They sat down on a bench just outside the shop, a street lamp throwing off a soft beam of light.

Addy licked her cone. Closed her eyes and savored. "Oh, my gosh, that's sinful."

"Worth every calorie, though."

"And then some. I'll be adding a few miles to my run tomorrow."

"How many miles do you do a week?"

"Thirty."

He raised an eyebrow. "Masochist."

"It's therapy. Give me six miles, I can usually work it out." She licked her cone again. "Most things, anyway."

"Mark fall under that umbrella?"

"A marathon wouldn't fix that," she said.

"Wanna talk about it?"

"There's nothing to talk about."

"Whatever happened between you two, you're not over it, are you?"

She fiddled with the paper around her waffle cone. "I'm over it," she said, a little defensive even to her own ears. "I just don't want to ever be in that place again."

He gave her a highly skeptical look. "So. How about that moon?"

She followed his glance skyward. "How did you and Liz meet?"

She'd turned the table, and the question surprised him. Clearly. "Sophomore year in college. At a party, ironically enough. Both of us on the other side of intoxicated." He hesitated, and then, "That was the first warning bell I ignored."

"What do you mean?"

He sighed a heavy sigh. "No one's told you?"

"I overheard a little something in the drugstore yesterday. Your friend Mae."

"Figures. So what'd you hear?"

"That she's in prison."

"Yeah." Silence and then, "She is."

"What happened?" Addy asked softly.

He was quiet for a moment, his expression serious. "She had a head-on with another car one afternoon on the way home from the grocery store.

Her blood alcohol was way over the legal limit, and Madeline was in the car."

"Oh, Culley," Addy said, the breath sticking in her throat.

"The other driver is paralyzed."

"How awful. Was Madeline hurt?"

"She had a couple broken bones. Thank God for car seats."

"Culley. I'm so sorry. What a horrible thing."

He dropped his ice cream into the trash can next to the bench. "It was pretty much a nightmare. Still is, I guess."

"Did you know there was a problem?"

"Hindsight's twenty-twenty. Liz always liked to have fun. In college, so did I. I went through the here-to-have-a-good-time major. When we started dating, we went to parties every night. I couldn't tell you how most of them ended. I got my own wake-up call when my grades started looking like they belonged to someone who was not going to med school."

"And Liz?"

He lifted a shoulder. "On the surface, she seemed to agree it was time to get serious. But there were nights when she would go out with the girls. They'd all get drunk, and even then, I knew something about it felt different."

"Did you tell her that?"

"Yeah, but she resented my calling her on it at all. Looking back, I can superimpose my dad's voice over her words. 'I don't have a problem. I'm making grades and having a little fun at night. What's so wrong with that?' I guess I didn't want to see, because from here, it all seems pretty clear. How could I have missed it?"

Addy's heart twisted. Many, many times when they were growing up, Culley had appeared at her house late at night, his eyes darkened by emotions she could not understand. She had known that his dad drank more than he should, that he got angry, yelled and threw things. As resentful as she was of her own father's defection, she'd thought she had it better than Culley. "I think sometimes we don't let ourselves see the things we don't want to see. Maybe until it's too late."

She got up, dropped the remainder of her ice cream in the trash can and sat back down.

Culley leaned against the bench, stared up at the night sky. "It was like being on this train where the brakes have failed. You know it's doomed. That there's only one ending. But you can't get off. So you just keep riding until all of a sudden, the train reaches the end of the line. That crash you've been fearing just happens in an instant. And you think to yourself I should have been able to do something to prevent it."

She put her hand on his forearm and squeezed. "That's where you're wrong. As much as we want to, we can't make other people's choices for them. We can tell them how we feel, but the ultimate decision is theirs."

"Is that true of what happened between you and Mark?"

Addy pulled her hand away, nodded. "And also the part about me not seeing what I apparently didn't want to see."

He didn't ask what she meant, and she was glad.

They were quiet for a good while. Just sat there on the bench, while something that felt comfortable and familiar settled over them. It was the way it had been before. Before the first time he'd kissed her when they were kids. Before Mark. Before. When they were young and could talk to each other about anything.

And since then, there had never been anyone else in her life with whom this had been true. She'd had Mark, friends, close friends like Ellen. But what she and Culley had been to one another all those years ago had been different.

She missed it with an intensity that wound a knot in her stomach.

And in recognizing its return, wanted to grab hold of it with both hands and never let go again.

"YOU LIKE HER, don't you?"

Culley had picked Madeline up from his mother's house and they were back on the main road, headed home when Madeline asked the question. Culley looked at his daughter, weighing his answer. "We were friends a long time ago."

"You like her as more than a friend now?" she asked without looking at him.

"Maybe," he said.

Madeline turned to stare out her window, even though it was dark. "Does she like you?"

"I don't know."

"Are you gonna marry her?"

The question threw him a curve. He pulled over to the side of the road, left his blinker on, turned to look at his daughter. "Hey," he said, reaching out to turn her chin toward him. "What's all this about?"

She lifted a shoulder, tipped her head to one side. "I saw the way you looked at her."

Culley ran the back of his hand across her hair. "You know what? I don't know what's going to happen. But there's one thing that's not going to change."

She looked up at him, her dark eyes troubled. "What?"

"How much I love you."

"How much?"

"Hmm." He pretended to think for a moment. It was a game they used to play. Hadn't played in three years. "As much as all the chocolate chips in all the cookies in the whole world."

She smiled. "And I love you as much as all the fish in all the oceans."

He put his arm around her, hugged her hard. When he pulled back, there were tears in her eyes. He wiped them away with his thumbs. "You know that's not ever going to change, right?"

She nodded. "We better get home," she said. "I have homework."

He pulled back onto the road, and she punched on a radio station. They drove the rest of the way in silence.

ADDY WAS DOWNSTAIRS the next morning, pouring a cup of coffee when the phone rang.

"Are you missing me enough to come back yet?" As usual, Ellen skipped the greeting.

"I miss you, yes," Addy said, glancing at the clock above the sink. Barely eight, but no doubt Ellen had been going strong for three hours or more.

"And are you bored to tears?"

"Actually, no."

"That have anything to do with house calls from the good doctor?"

Addy smiled. "No."

"But you've seen him."

"A little."

"What does that mean?"

"We're friends."

"Oh." Disappointment dripped from Ellen's voice.

"We both decided being friends made a lot more sense."

"Both decided or you decided?"

"He agreed. Sort of." With the assertion came a clip of memory from last night and the feel of Culley's hand on her arm.

"But that night in New York wasn't about being friends, was it?"

"That was different."

"How so?"

"That was a mistake."

"At least you got to have some fun while you were making it."

"Ellen."

"Well, seriously, Addy, how long are you going to keep Mark in the picture?"

"He's not in the picture."

"Oh, really."

"Yes, really."

"Not from where I'm sitting."

"And what is the view from there?"

"A thirty-three-year-old divorced woman scared to death of putting herself out there again."

"I'm out there."

Ellen laughed. "Yeah, out in the boonies. But if you have to be there, at least give the good doctor a chance. Remember, careful gets you a lot of boring nights at home alone."

"It also keeps you from making a fool of yourself."

"Ah. So that's it. Wounded pride."

"It's not that simple."

"Or that complicated. Addy, you're letting Mark win, you know. That's a lot of glory to give someone who surely doesn't deserve it."

From there, they talked about work for a bit. Ellen had a few questions on some of the cases she'd taken over for her. When they were done, Addy clicked the phone off, placed it on the kitchen counter. Was Ellen right? Did Mark still have a hold on her?

Maybe it was true. But if it was also true that people are shaped by the events in their lives, she had surely been irrevocably changed by the discovery that her perception of her marriage had no basis whatsoever in reality.

It *was* time to move on. She knew this, and yet, her feet were planted in cement. Moving on meant taking a chance on her own judgment again. Getting past that picture she carried around in her head of Mark in their bed with another woman, a woman who had carried his child.

She wanted to get over it. She just didn't know if she ever would.

ADDY AND CLAIRE spent the next two days going through the accounts for the orchard, looking at where money was going out, how much was coming in. The problem lay in the fact that there was far more of the former than the latter.

Addy could not fault her mother. It seemed that she was right. Over the years, the market had continued to tighten, competition intensifying with the availability of produce from other countries such as Mexico and Canada. Taylor Orchards had once been the primary vendor for three of the major grocery chains in Virginia and North Carolina. That was no longer the case.

For the past decade, their share of the market pie had continued to decrease until, based on the numbers, it was clear to Addy that selling out might be the wisest choice.

Claire said as much at the end of their second day at the kitchen table. She ran a hand through her hair and said, "There's nothing wrong with making a graceful exit, honey. All things come to an end. That's just part of the life cycle. No business can go on forever."

"But it's been in your family since your grandma and grandpa."

"And it's had a good run." She sighed. "I'm okay with letting it go."

Addy stared at the papers sitting in neat stacks on the table, bills, receipts, invoices, all evidence of Claire's hard work. Was her mother right? Was it time to declare defeat, acknowledge that like people, times changed? Bow out gracefully?

Judging from the evidence in front of her, the answer was a clear one.

But in the short time she'd been back, a subtle shift had taken place inside Addy. She'd arrived at the orchard feeling like a stranger who had once lived here. With each passing day, her love for the place rose a little higher inside her like the tide creeping back into shore. And she wanted it to thrive again.

LATER THAT NIGHT, Addy went down to the barn to check on the fawn, gave her some carrots which had quickly become a favorite. Back at the house, she settled into a leather chair in the living room with her laptop, logging onto the Internet.

Claire had already gone up, saying she was tired. Addy had watched her climb the stairs, hearing a new note in her mother's voice that she was sure had more to do with resignation than fatigue.

She used a search engine to locate the Web pages for some of their major competitors. Most of them big commercial producers, they all had impressive sites.

She then poked around for studies on the marketing of produce. Found several. She was reading through the third one when a car pulled up outside.

She started across the floor to see who it was just as a crash reverberated through the room. Glass flew. Addy jumped back, a shard catching the inside of her right calf.

A rock landed on top of her computer, smashing the keyboard. Addy stared for a moment, too shocked to move. She bolted to the window, but the car had already roared backwards and peeled off down the driveway.

Claire clattered down the stairs, calling out, "Addy, what is it? What happened?"

"Someone threw a rock through the window," she said, still stunned.

"Oh, my goodness," Claire said. "You're bleeding."

Addy looked down, saw a circle of blood pooling on the floor beside her.

Claire took her arm, led her to the couch. "Let me see how bad it is."

The cut was jagged and bleeding at a fairly alarming rate.

"I'll get the first-aid kit," Claire said, heading for the kitchen.

She was back in a few moments with the phone tucked under her chin, talking. "Ida, I'm so glad you're there. Is Culley home?"

Addy waved both hands to stop her.

"Oh, good. Addy's been hurt. Could you please ask him to run over?"

Addy dropped her head back against the couch. "I wish you hadn't done that. I'm fine."

"I'll feel better if he looks at it. And I know he won't mind." She pulled some gauze from the kit and pressed it to the wound. "Where's the rock?"

"It rolled under the desk."

"Keep pressure on this," Claire said. She found

the grapefruit-size rock, held it up. "There's a note attached."

"What does it say?"

Claire unfolded the paper. "'One way or another, the interstate will go through Lindmore County. Warning: that little fire was a test run.'"

Addy sat there for a moment. "Who would do this?"

"I have no idea."

Headlights arced through the window. Footsteps sounded on the porch and then a knock. "Addy? Claire?"

Culley. Claire went to let him in, and Addy had to admit she was relieved to see him. He crossed the living room in a few swift strides, dropping to one knee beside her and setting a leather medical bag down on the floor.

"What happened?" he asked.

"I think someone was trying to make a point," Addy said.

Claire held up the rock and handed him the note. He read it with a frown. He pulled back the gauze on Addy's leg, then opened his bag and removed a jar of some kind of ointment. He opened a pack of gauze. "It's a fairly clean slice. It won't need stitches. But it'll be pretty sore for a couple of days."

Addy nodded.

"Have you called the sheriff?"

"No," Claire said. "Maybe we should just let it go."

"The next time it could be something far worse, Mama. We need to let the authorities handle it."

"She's right, Claire," Culley agreed, his voice respectful but insistent.

With reluctance, Claire dialed the sheriff's office while Culley cleaned Addy's cut with something that stung.

"Sorry," he said. "It shouldn't last long."

Claire stepped out into the foyer, telling the officer on duty what had happened.

"I'm sorry Mama called you over here."

"I'm not." He looked up, met her gaze with a smile that could melt an ice cube. "That's what friends are for, right?"

CHAPTER ELEVEN

SHERIFF RAMSEY ARRIVED a few minutes later along with two of his deputies. They asked Claire and Addy for their versions of what had happened.

There wasn't much to tell. Neither of them had seen anything. He assured them they would do their best to find out who did it, but the look on his face was doubtful.

"I was just over at Oscar Hammond's place this morning," the sheriff said. "Somebody had slashed the tires on all his farm equipment. He got the same kind of note."

"Who could be so desperate to have this interstate go through?" Claire asked.

"I wish I knew. That would give us our answer, wouldn't it?"

It was nearly ten o'clock by the time Sheriff Ramsey and his deputies left. Culley had gone out to the barn and found some plywood to nail over the window until they could call someone to fix the broken glass.

He came back in the house and said, "Not exactly a beautiful piece of workmanship, but it should keep the bugs out."

"Thank you, Culley," Claire said. "If you two don't mind, I'm going up to bed. I'm a little beat."

"Are you all right, Mama?" Addy asked.

"I'm fine. I'll see you in the morning. Thank you again, Culley," she said on the way up the stairs.

"Anytime."

The two of them stood in the foyer. Claire's bedroom door clicked closed, echoing in the silence.

"I'd better get going, too," he said. "Leg okay?"

"Yes. Thank you. I'll walk you out."

Outside, the sky was sprinkled with stars, a half moon hung high. Culley set his bag inside the Explorer, then turned with one hand on the door. "You'll be okay?"

"Yes." She folded her arms across her chest.

"They'll find who did it, eventually."

She nodded. "I know."

"I'm glad you're all right."

There was more than simple politeness behind his words. And she was at once glad and grateful to know that he was here.

He reached out, brushed the back of his hand against hers, a feather touch, then threaded his fingers through hers and tugged her to him. He had his back to the vehicle, feet apart. She stood between his legs, her gaze set on the buttons of his shirt.

She should really step back, stop this now before it went any further. But the desire to see if memory had touched up the reality of that night in New York was strong.

One kiss.

What could it hurt?

And then he kissed her, swift and swooping, as if not giving either of them a chance to change their mind.

Just then, it was the last thing that would have occurred to her.

Memory had done a fine job of holding on to the details. It was one of those kisses that hits the bloodstream like a drug, instant ignition. Everything inside her went weak, and at the same time was empowered with something so good and real that she wanted to freeze the moment, prevent it from melting away.

He pulled back, and they looked at one another again, acknowledging the impact of the kiss.

He fit a hand to either side of her waist, bringing her up flush against him. And they settled into another kiss that had a little less fire at its center, but no less potency.

"You know, this friendship thing—" he said, his lips at the corner of her mouth.

She tipped her head to the side. "Umm."

"It's not so bad if kissing like that is a part of it."

"Yeah." The word came out on an exhale. "So...you think being friends doesn't mean we can't kiss."

"It's working for me." This while he nuzzled the soft spot beneath her ear, his hand dropping from her waist to the back of her hip.

It was getting harder to think, much less breathe.

She dropped her head back and then stepped away. "Go home, Culley Rutherford."

He looked at her, a too-appealing half smile accompanying his, "You sure?"

She took another step back, needing distance for clarity. "Yeah. I'm sure." *Weak, Addy.* Even to her own ears.

He swung the door open, slid onto the seat. "Promise me something?"

"Maybe."

"Leave this as it is? Don't spend the next two hours adding a whole bunch of what-now's to it. Let's just let it be what it is."

"And what is it?" she asked softly.

"A few pretty hot kisses between two people who used to like each other. And still do."

He closed the door, and she stood there, arms folded across her chest, watching as he lifted a hand, backed up, then rolled off down the driveway.

CULLEY LET HIMSELF into the house a few minutes later. His mom was waiting in the foyer.

"Madeline asleep?" he asked.

"Yes. I read her some books, and she drifted off on the last one."

"Thanks, Mom."

"How's Addy?"

"She had a pretty good gash on her leg."

"Thank goodness it wasn't worse."

They went into the kitchen. Ida poured him a glass of tea from the pitcher on the counter, then added some ice. "All right if I make an unasked for observation?"

"It's pretty certain you're going to whether I say yes or not," he said with an indulgent smile.

"It's been good for you, having Addy here. I see something of who you used to be." Ida patted him on the shoulder and nodded.

After she had left, Culley took his tea to the office off the living room. He sat down in the leather chair and thought about what his mom had said.

Over the years, he had changed. He'd once been a guy who knew how to have fun. His outlook on life one in which he saw the glass half-full. His marriage to Liz had eroded all that, until the result was somebody he didn't like being. A guy who worked too much, saw his daughter too little, smiled infrequently enough that she looked surprised when he did.

Tonight, standing under a sky filled with stars, he'd kissed the woman with whom he'd actually once shared a baby pool. And realized that he wanted to be who he'd once been. A guy who could admit his life hadn't taken the path he'd envisioned. But could move on.

He opened his eyes and sat up. That was the difference. For the first time in three years, he wanted to move on. Make a new beginning.

The cell phone on the desk rang. He glanced at the caller ID, didn't recognize the number but picked it up. "Hello."

"Hey. It's me."

He sat back in the chair, pressed two fingers to the bridge of his nose. "Liz."

"I'm in the infirmary with some kind of stomach bug. There's a nice nurse here who snuck me a phone."

"Oh," he said.

There was a heavy pause, as if they had no idea what to say to one another. Which, on his part, was true.

"Did you get the letter I sent a while back?"

"Yes," he said, feeling a stab of guilt for not having responded.

"Can you come for a visit, Culley?"

Culley squeezed his eyes shut. Even though they were no longer married, no matter how hard he tried to convince himself that Liz's life was her own now, he still felt sorry for her.

"You don't owe me anything, Culley," she said, her voice dropping a few notes. "I'm just scared."

"Liz," he said, the hard knot in his voice softening. "I want to see this end so you can get on with your life. But you understand that's what it will be, don't you? You getting on with your life."

"I know you've moved on. Beyond what our divorce papers say. And I don't blame you."

He heard the loneliness in her voice, marked as it was by an edge of desperation. Was it so much to ask, really? They hadn't seen one another in a long time; the last few times he'd taken Madeline, his mom had gone in to supervise the visit. He hadn't wanted to see Liz.

Another shaft of guilt hit him for that. Maybe it would be the right thing, to go. Give them both some closure. "All right," he said. "I'll come on Monday."

"Thank you, Culley. I'll see you then."

He disconnected the phone. Sat there for a while thinking about Addy and what it had been like kissing her tonight. Of how he'd driven home feeling like he'd been filled with helium.

He compared that to how he felt now. As if all the curtains had been drawn, and the room was pitch-black, the air inside stale.

He didn't want to feel that way anymore. He wanted his life to be one in which the windows were wide open, a breeze stirring.

The clock struck midnight, and with it came a sudden resolve. He would go see Liz on Monday. And then close the door for good.

NIGHTTIME WAS THE WORST.

Liz Rutherford lay on the narrow bunk, staring at the ceiling. Below her, the woman with whom she'd shared the bleak cell since her incarceration, snored softly. She was in on a child-abuse conviction.

At night, when they were both lying in bed,

wishing for sleep, regret hung over the room like a thick fog. Liz wondered if either of them would ever see past it.

That was the hard part about being in this place. She had all the time in the world to reflect on the wrongs she'd done, and yet she couldn't do anything about trying to fix it. Not that any of it was fixable. She'd tossed her marriage out the window, put her daughter's life in jeopardy, paralyzed a man.

All for a bottle of booze.

Sometimes, lying here thinking about what had happened, it felt as if it must have been someone else's life. That she couldn't possibly have done what she had.

But no matter how many times she circled it, that was the point she always came back to. She had done those horrible things.

On the heels of that came another hope. Maybe there was still time. Maybe it wasn't too late to make things right. Culley had agreed to visit. That was something. A glimmer of light to cling to.

She rolled over on her side, pressed her face into the pillow. He had given her so many chances. But that was Culley. He'd believed in her, thought she could turn her back on the drinking, rise above it. Put her family first.

But the need had gone deeper than that. Deeper

than anything in her life. As ashamed as she was to admit it, deeper than her love for her husband or her child.

That was the part that scared her most about leaving this place. She'd been through the treatment program, of course, hadn't had a sip of alcohol since she'd entered the prison. But out there? What about when she got out?

She held her hand up in the near dark. It shook.

CULLEY AWOKE TO the sound of sobbing.

At first he thought he was dreaming. He lay there in the dark for a moment, straining to hear.

Madeline.

Wide-awake now, he swung out of bed and lunged down the hall. He opened her door, stepped into the room. "Madeline?" he called out quietly.

She lay on her side, facing away from him. And she was crying as he'd never heard her cry before, heartwrenching sobs that sounded as if they came from some wounded spot deep inside her. He flicked on the lamp, sat down on the edge of the bed, rubbing a hand across her hair. "Honey? What is it?"

She turned to look at him then, bolted upright and locked her arms around his neck, as if she were drowning, and he was the only buoy in sight.

She pressed her face to his chest, the sobs coming harder now. He cradled her to him, stroking her hair and letting her cry.

When her sobs began to soften, he pulled back and said, "What's wrong, baby?"

"I had a dream. An awful dream."

"About what?"

She looked down, shook her head. "It doesn't matter."

"It does matter," he said, tipping her chin up so that she was forced to look at him. Her eyes were red-rimmed and puffy, her lashes glistening with tears. "To me, it matters."

She was quiet for a while, her crying turning to snuffles. "It was about the accident."

"Oh, sweetie."

She hesitated, and then, "I—I was trapped in the car. I couldn't get out, and I kept calling to Mama, but she wouldn't wake up. She didn't hear me."

Culley pulled her tight against him again, his chest aching with fresh sorrow, regret. "You were dreaming, honey. It's just a dream."

"But that's how it happened," she said, pulling back to look up at him with urgent eyes. "I kept calling and calling. And she wouldn't wake up. I could see the other car through the windshield, and that man was screaming."

Culley cupped her cheek with his hand, pain searing through him. She had never talked about it before. Had never wanted to. He had assumed she didn't remember. Or didn't want to. "I'm so sorry, honey."

She launched herself at him again, wrapping her arms around him and holding on as if she never wanted to let go. "It was so awful, Daddy."

He held her, stroked her hair, wishing for words to comfort her, wishing he could wipe that day from their past as if it had never happened. "I'm so sorry," he said again because it was true even if it didn't make it better.

A MEETING HAD been scheduled in town on Saturday during which Congressman Bill Powers was scheduled to address the citizens of Harper's Mill with his view on why the new interstate would be a positive boon to the county.

Addy and Claire drove in together, pulling up outside the community center just before seven o'clock.

The meeting room was full. Lowell Duncan, the town mayor, called the meeting to order behind a microphone that squawked when he spoke into it. He stepped back, smiled and tapped it a couple times, then spoke again.

"Good evening, everyone. You all know why we're here tonight. One of the proposed routes for Interstate 92 plows a path right through the heart of our county. Many of you have homes and businesses that will be directly affected. At the table to my left, we have several representatives from the Virginia Department of Transportation as well as Congressman Bill Powers. Congressman Powers, if you would like to speak first, then we'll open the floor up to discussion."

A short man with a big voice, Congressman Powers removed the microphone from its stand and stepped out from behind the podium. "I'm very pleased to be here tonight, although I'm sure most of you would prefer that it be for another reason. This is not the easiest point to make, and certainly not the most popular, but I believe that what is in the best interest of many sometimes involves the sacrifice of a few. The proposed route for Corridor A would bring about a good bit of change in this county, but the studies show that the resulting creation of new businesses would actually be a major economic boost to the area."

The congressman continued on for another twenty minutes, during which the mood of the crowd did not soften. Addy looked around at the people who sat with folded arms and straight backs, their faces set in disapproval.

The congressman concluded with a pitch aimed at the greater good.

Mayor Duncan stepped forward. "Thank you, Congressman. We'll now take questions and comments."

Addy and Claire were seated in the middle of the room. All around them, people raised their hands, wanting a turn to speak. Things heated up fast. Over a hundred homes would be bulldozed should this route be chosen, one of them with documents dating back to 1769 and a land grant from King George III of England. There was history in the community, and people didn't want to see it replaced with truck stops.

After the fifth person had spoken, Addy leaned over and whispered to her mother, "Aren't you going to say something?"

"I hadn't planned to."

"You should."

Claire shook her head and then, "Oh, why not?" She raised her hand.

Mayor Duncan nodded and said, "Claire?"

Claire stood, cleared her throat. "Both my home and business stand to be destroyed if this proposal goes through. I realize that wherever the road is built, someone will lose something they value. And I understand that some people think the economic growth stimulated by such a road would offset the loss to people like me. That very well may be true, but that doesn't change the fact that I love my home. My grandparents started Taylor Orchard in the twenties. Times are a little hard right now, but it would be very painful to see the efforts of generations of my family bulldozed and paved over as if they were never there. I know that's true for others in this room as well." She sat down.

"Thank you, Claire," the mayor said.

Addy squeezed her mother's hand. Claire squeezed back.

The door opened in the back of the room. Addy glanced over her shoulder. Culley stood just inside the entrance. He lifted a hand. She raised a hand back, glad to see him in a way that said a lot of things that were hard to deny.

The discussion went on for another hour, during which Claire's sentiments were echoed again and again. Mayor Duncan thanked everyone for coming and called the meeting to a close. People stood in clusters talking, Claire stepping aside to speak to some of the ladies from church.

Addy made her way to the back of the room where Culley stood waiting.

"Hi," he said.

"Hi. I didn't know you were coming."

"I wanted to be here at the beginning, but I had an emergency at the office."

"Everything all right?"

"Should be. Walk you outside?"

She nodded.

The night was warm, the sky just beginning to darken. They stood by the entrance, while the crowd from the meeting streamed out. Most of them offered up friendly hellos. "Evening, Dr. Rutherford. Addy."

"People like you here, don't they?" Addy said.

"I like the people here, so it's mutual." He studied her for a moment. "Can I drive you home?"

She hesitated, debated the wisdom of it. She realized, though, that she wanted to go. "Let me just go tell Mama."

"I'll wait here."

A few minutes later, they were headed out of town, down some country roads she hadn't been on in years. They looped through the county, taking whichever turns suited them, just driving.

"Do you think the meeting went well?" she asked.

"I don't know. Powers seems pretty determined. But there was a lot of emotion in there tonight. That has to mean something."

"I hope so," she said. "I believe in progress. And I know things have to change sometimes. But it's not always worth the price."

They ended up at the municipal baseball field, a place where all the teenagers used to hang out when they were in school. Culley parked the car, and they got out, leaning against the front of the Explorer.

"Now this brings back some memories," Addy said.

"Can you still hit like a boy?" he asked, grinning.

She leaned back, chastising, "Chauvinistic and beneath you."

"Well, you did hit better than most of the boys."

"True."

He pointed to the sky. "What a great night for a telescope."

"You used to be into astronomy."

"Back when I thought it would be great to live somewhere else, even another planet. Anywhere but under my dad's roof."

Addy heard the forced lightness in his voice, but knew there was truth behind the words. She put her hand over his, squeezed once.

He looked at her, started to speak, stopped, then said, "Liz called last night. She asked me to come see her."

Addy blinked, not sure what to say. "Is she all right?"

"She's going to be released soon."

"That's good, isn't it?" she asked softly.

"I think so. She seems remorseful. I know she never meant to do what she did." He drew in a deep breath, then blew it out. "I've wished so many times I could snap my fingers and change what happened. Roll back the tape and put her somewhere so that she was forced to give up the drinking. But I can't do that. And now I just want it to end. This feeling responsible for her. That's terrible, isn't it?"

Addy reached out, put a hand on his arm. "I'd say it's a part of who you are. An admirable part of who you are."

"I don't feel admirable. More like resentful. Like the ball and chain she's tied to herself is tied to me, too."

"What will she do when she gets out?"

"I don't know."

"Do you think she'll start drinking again?"

"Madeline asked me the same thing." He looked down, let out a heavy, burdened sigh. "She had a nightmare last night. About the accident. It was the first time she's ever talked about it. I've gotta tell you, it pretty much tore my heart out."

"Was she okay?"

"After a while, yeah. And maybe it was actually good that it surfaced. I've worried all along that she'd put that day away and refused to look at it. Maybe now, she can start to let that part of it go. But I think she's worried about what's going to happen to her mother."

They stood for a while, the silence between them comfortable in a way that Addy might have found stilted with someone else.

"Can I ask you something?"

"Sure," she said.

"You think there's a reason why we're in each other's life again after all these years?"

She bit her lip. "I don't know."

He reached out, ran a finger across her hair. "I've walked around these last three years feeling like there was this big hole inside me. And since that night in New York, that hole has felt like it's getting smaller."

She had no idea what to say. They were headed down a path she'd declared she had no intention of taking. And yet, here she was, wishing again that he would kiss her.

Which he did now. Thoroughly. The kind of

kiss that melts any resolve to remain clear-headed. The kind of kiss that goes on for a while and ends with reluctance.

A half smile touched the corner of his mouth. "I always wanted to take you parking," he said.

Addy gave him a look. "Like you could have fit me in. Your Friday and Saturday nights were booked."

"Were not."

"Were, too."

"So what would it have been like? The two of us. If Mark hadn't come into the picture, I mean."

She'd wondered herself. Many times. "Probably never would have worked."

"Why?"

"You dated cheerleaders."

"And you're going to hold that against me?"

"Just making my case."

"I can offer evidence to the contrary, counselor."

"Proceed."

He leaned in, kissed her again.

She could have attempted indifference, but the performance would have fallen flat. It was pretty much out of the question when a man kissed like that.

Several minutes later, she said, "Okay, so point made."

He smiled. "What do you think about a date to-morrow night?"

"What kind of date?"

"A real date. The kind where I come to your front door, pick you up and we go to dinner or a movie."

"What happened to the friends thing?"

He looked at her for a long moment. "That kind of feels like it would be settling."

She could think of a dozen reasons to say no, each of them valid. But Ellen's voice popped into her head. *You're letting Mark win.*

"Okay," she said. "What time should I be ready?"

CHAPTER TWELVE

ADDY FELT LIKE a teenager. She'd changed clothes a half-dozen times before finally settling on a pair of black Capri pants and a halter-style Gap T-shirt.

Culley picked her up at six-thirty, and his response when she opened the door was the one a girl hopes for.

A long stare, and then, "You look amazing."

She smiled. "You look pretty great yourself."

He wore blue jeans and a white shirt that emphasized his well-shaped shoulders. Throughout the day, she'd repeated her resolve to remain levelheaded about what this night would be. But attraction had its own agenda, and she couldn't deny that the friendship pact was not holding water.

In fact, it was sinking fast. Being redefined by something over which she was beginning to think she had little control.

They drove thirty miles to Roanoke, ate dinner downtown at an upscale restaurant that featured

American-style cuisine. The walls were paneled in mahogany. Sconce lighting gave the place an immediate feeling of intimacy. They sat in a booth in one corner of the restaurant, drank red wine that rolled smoothly on their tongues.

The food was wonderful. Addy ordered a tomato and mozzarella salad with basil and aged balsamic vinegar. It was so good she could have made that her entire meal. For two hours, they ate and talked. About everything, one topic weaving itself into another, college and work, Madeline's already blooming talent for drawing, Addy's concern that Sheriff Ramsey had not yet established a credible lead as to who was behind the threats against Claire and others in the community opposed to the route leading through Lindmore County.

"I heard Owen Blankenship's hay barn was set on fire early this morning," Culley said. "Took out a winter's worth of round bales."

"He's got the big dairy farm on Route 638, right?"

"Yeah. Owen's been pretty vocal about his opposition. He's taken out some ads in the paper. Even challenged Congressman Powers to a public debate. Owen's another landowner who would see his property sliced in half. Not too desirable to have half your cows on one side of the interstate and half on the other."

"Are they sure this was related to that?"

Culley nodded. "Apparently, this one came with a threat to his family."

Addy felt the color leave her face.

"Whoever's behind it is serious."

"So short of selling out without a fight, what can we do?"

"They'll mess up at some point. They're getting too brazen."

"I just hope it's sooner rather than later. I think I'll call home and make sure everything is okay." She pulled her cell phone from her purse. Claire answered on the first ring, assured her there was no reason to worry and that she shouldn't give it another thought.

"I have a feeling if anyone shows up there again, Claire's going to be ready for them," Culley said. "She still have that old .22?"

"Yeah. Not the most powerful gun, but she could do some damage."

Culley smiled. "Remember the time she ran off Wimmer Brown when he accused us of stealing from his ice-cream truck?"

She nodded, and then they both laughed. "That old truck probably hit sixty going down the driveway."

They went on to other topics, old memories and new stuff, too, careers, aspirations, disappointments.

Growing up, the two of them had been able to talk to each other about anything. They still could, and it was something she had missed. She and Mark had reached a point where they couldn't talk about anything. Couldn't. Or wouldn't.

"Do you ever miss your marriage?" she asked, rubbing a thumb around the rim of her wineglass.

He considered the question for a moment, then, "I miss being married. I'm not into the singles scene. Some of my buddies wax poetic about what they'd do if they had their freedom back, but it's not what they think it is."

Addy made a gesture of agreement. "My friend Ellen in D.C. has been divorced for about five years. I've listened to enough of her dating horror stories to know I'm content to stand on the sidelines."

"It's not that easy to meet someone. There are a lot of desperate people out there."

"I think Ellen has dated most of them."

He smiled.

She tapped a thumb on the edge of her plate, reaching for honesty even though she knew it would leave her vulnerable. "I feel like I have this shield around myself now, and the thought of letting someone past it…frankly, terrifies me."

Culley's expression was somber now. He didn't say anything for a few moments, and then said, "You put your trust in someone you loved, and he let you down."

She was quiet for a moment. "It's like I'd been following this one particular road map all those years, and then I wake up to realize I'm in a completely different place than I had thought. And my map is all wrong."

He reached across the table, took her hand. "He's just one man who obviously didn't realize what he had. The whole world's not going to treat you that way, Addy."

She swiped the back of her hand across her cheek, embarrassed by the sudden tears. "I hate how much it still hurts."

"I hate that he hurt you."

"I wish I could snap my fingers and make it go away."

"I don't think it works that way. When someone lets you down, it's like having your feet knocked from under you. It takes time to believe you can get up and actually start walking around again. I know that from my own life."

Addy looked at him, saw the understanding in his eyes, felt the forging of a new bond between them. "So maybe that night in New York was a stroke of luck. Or fate. Do you believe in that?" she asked softly.

"I believe we have threads in our lives that are sometimes left hanging. That if we're lucky we get an opportunity to follow through on them."

"And you think we're one of those threads?"

He gave her a long, assessing look, his eyes warm and intense. "Yeah. I guess I do."

She had tried these past weeks to keep her feelings for Culley in a box small enough that she could deny their existence. But the box was splitting at the corners, the sides no longer able to contain the simple fact that she was happy when they were together. Happy. And just that was enough to make her wonder if it was time to see what they could be. To stick her head out of her shell and discover what the world could look like if she allowed herself to see it through new eyes.

They decided to split dessert. It arrived at their table on an oversize plate, a warm chocolate cake drizzled with a white chocolate sauce.

Addy dipped her spoon in, closed her eyes and savored. "Umm. Oh, that's good."

He tasted it. "If I eat more than three bites, stab me with your fork."

Addy laughed. "More for me."

They took their time driving back. He had FM

radio in his car, and she found a station that played hits from the eighties. Fleetwood Mac. Foreigner. The Cars. The songs brought back memories of hot summer days when they would ride their bikes out to the pond at the edge of the orchard and sun themselves on the dock, eating tomato sandwiches they'd packed in a cooler and drinking lemonade out of mason jars.

Addy felt like she was in high school again, wishing for the ride home to take longer than it should. Too soon, Culley pulled into her driveway, cut the engine. He had the sunroof open, and Addy dropped her head against the seat, looking up at the sky. He reached for her hand, threaded his fingers through hers. They sat that way for a minute or two before she said, "So what is this?"

"Us?"

"Yeah, us."

"You sure you want to define it right now? Because I have a feeling if we do, you're going to run. And I think it scares you to death that this might be something other than what you've already labeled it."

She laced her fingers together. "We have history. I don't know. I guess I don't want to mess that up."

"To me, that history feels like a beginning. As

if we have a whole foundation of knowledge of one another."

She smiled. "So where did I bury my first lost tooth?"

"Under the oldest boxwood in your yard. Your theory was that if the tooth fairy were real, she'd be able to find it there."

"I still think it was a good theory."

"Yeah, but you didn't get your dollar."

"True."

They sat there, studying each other, letting the feelings swirling between them sink and settle.

"I'm thirty-three years old," Culley said after a few moments. "I'm supposed to have all the moves down. But I swear when I'm with you, Addy, I feel like I'm seventeen again, and I just want to get it right."

He leaned close then, settled a kiss on her mouth. It was sweet and stirring, everything a good-night kiss should be. Through the open windows of the car, a night breeze feathered through.

They kissed for a good while, just taking their time with it, as if the destination weren't the important thing, but the journey itself.

When he finally pulled back, he ran a thumb under the curve of her jaw. "Being friends has its plusses, but none of them compare to kissing you."

It would have been a waste of time to try and convince herself she didn't enjoy hearing that. "Okay, so you're a pretty good kisser," she said.

He held up a hand. "Stop. The flattery. Too much."

She laughed. "You're a great kisser. There, satisfied?"

"Mollified."

"You're just used to women like Mae Carter going weak in the knees when you look their way."

"At least twice a day."

She shook her head.

"So. Are we dating?" he asked.

"Dating. Strong word."

"How about seeing each other?"

"Leaves room for interpretation."

"A necessity."

"How about let's just see where it goes?"

He tipped his head to one side, lifted a shoulder. "Yeah. Okay."

"I had a really good time," she said.

"So did I. I'll call you?"

She nodded once, opened her door. "I'm going now."

"Walk you to the porch?"

"You'll just try to kiss me again."

"At least you know me."

"Good night, Culley," she said, smiling.

"Good night, Addy."

At the front porch steps, she turned and watched the taillights of his SUV disappear around the bend. It couldn't be this easy, could it? Two people finding something that felt this good after surviving something that initially had not felt survivable.

It was scary to think that it might just be that easy. And maybe cowardly not to give it a chance.

ADDY SPENT THE following day on the tractor, mowing up and down the lanes between the apple trees. The to-do list was seemingly endless. She had no idea how her mother had kept everything going with the amount of help she had. Addy had placed an ad in the paper for a full-time position, but so far had no responses.

It had been years since she had been on a tractor. She took her time at first, then gradually got comfortable enough to increase the speed. Claire brought chicken-salad sandwiches and iced tea at noon, and they ate in the shade.

"Sheriff Ramsey called," Claire said. "They think they have a lead on the car that was here the other night. Apparently, the same car was spotted leaving Owen Blankenship's place just before the barn fire."

"I really hope they find them before they do something else."

"They will." Claire gave Addy a long look, before adding, "So. Are you and Culley an item now?"

Addy took a sip of her tea, unable to meet her mother's gaze. "I'm not sure what we are."

"Whatever it is, it's having a nice effect on you."

"Whatever it is, we're having a good time."

LATER THAT AFTERNOON, Addy arrived back at the house, gritty, her ponytail drooping on one side. Sweat stains marked the armpits and back of her blue sleeveless T-shirt. Her jeans had a grease stain from leaning up against the tractor when a branch had gotten stuck under the Bush Hog. She longed for a cool shower.

She parked the tractor in the shed next to the barn and headed to the house. A dark blue BMW convertible sat in the driveway, the top down. A man stood on the porch talking to her mother.

Addy's stomach dropped as recognition hit her. Mark. What was he doing here? Her first thought was to turn and leave. But he spotted her before she could act on it.

He was dressed in suit pants and a white shirt, a tie loose at his throat. He looked as if he'd lost weight, and there were shadows beneath his eyes.

"Hello, Addy," he said.

"What are you doing here?"

"Could we talk?"

Claire cleared her throat. "I'll be inside. Would you like something to drink, Mark?"

"He won't be staying that long, Mama."

"No, thank you, Claire. I'm fine."

Claire nodded and opened the screen door, closing it behind her.

He aimed a glance at the tractor she'd just parked. "That what you gave up practicing law for?"

"Why are you here?" Addy asked.

He sat down in a white wicker chair, leaned forward, elbows on his knees. "I've missed you, Addy."

She stared at him for a long moment, surprise robbing her of a response. "You're not serious, are you?"

"Completely."

She dropped her head back and counted to five. "The last I heard you were the father of a baby boy. And your twenty-something lover had moved in with you."

He dropped his gaze to the porch floor. "It's not working out that great."

"And you came here for sympathy?" She ushered a hand toward his car. "Let me save you some time. You came to the wrong place."

"I didn't come here for that."

"Then what?"

"I came to see you."

"I can't think of a single logical reason why that would be."

"Because we used to be able to talk."

She anchored her arms around her chest. "What is it you want to talk about?"

"Us."

"There is no us."

He ran a hand through his hair, his expression one of complete misery. "Addy, I'm sorry. God, I'm sorry."

There. The words she'd wanted so very much in the beginning, wished that he could say and mean. She believed him. She heard the truth of it in his voice. And yet, the words rang empty inside her. Because what did they fix? They didn't change anything that had happened.

"You didn't need to come all the way here to tell me that. It's too late for apologies."

He stood, crossed the porch floor and stopped a few inches from her. He reached out and brushed the back of his hand across her hair. "I know," he said. "What I did was horrible. If I could do things over again—"

She held up a hand to stop him. "Don't, Mark."

He tipped her chin up, forced her to look at him. "Can you honestly say you don't feel anything for me?"

She didn't answer right away, but took the moment to give the question its due.

A car rolled up. Addy looked over her shoulder. Culley. She took a step back.

He got out, lifted a hand. "Hello, Mark."

Mark nodded. "Culley."

"I'll come back later, Addy," Culley said.

"No. Stay. Mark was just leaving."

Mark looked at the two of them for a moment. "So it's true, then?"

Addy stared at him, incredulous. "Is that why you came here? Because you thought Culley and I were seeing each other?"

He dropped a guilty glance at the porch floor. Then looked at Culley with something very like resentment on his face. "You probably couldn't wait until the ink on the divorce papers had dried, could you?"

Culley gave him a narrow look. "It wasn't like that, Mark."

"Yeah, right. You think I didn't know back in high school that she was the one you wanted."

"It didn't matter what I wanted. She was with you."

"Oh, yeah. Mr. Loyal."

"You wouldn't know anything about the meaning of the word, Mark," Addy said, angry now.

Culley walked up to the bottom step of the porch. "Maybe you ought to go somewhere and cool off."

Mark raised both hands in the air. "And leave the field wide open for you, Rutherford? It looks like you've already cleared yourself a nice path. Make sure you tell her every bad thing you can remember about me. And don't leave anything out. Those road trips we took. The wedding weekend."

Something heavy settled in Addy's stomach. "Mark, go," she said.

He swung around, his eyes narrowed. "I'm going. I don't know what I was thinking to come here."

Addy stood there on the top step of the porch, her arms wrapped around herself, as if she could hold the questions banging at her chest inside. Mark got in the car, backed up and drove away.

Culley looked at her, concern in his eyes. "Are you okay?"

She nodded, not moving, just staying there in that same spot.

He stepped forward and touched her arm. "Here, sit," he said.

She sat down on the top step, planted an elbow on one knee, ran a hand through her hair. "Are you going to tell me what he meant by that?"

"Addy—"

"I didn't know him at all, did I?" Disbelief laced her voice. "How can that be? How could I have been married to someone for eleven years and think he was something completely different from what he was?"

Culley reached out to touch her, but she pulled away.

"Tell me what happened."

"Addy—"

"I want to know. Tell me."

He stared up at the sky for a long moment. "This isn't my place."

"I'm asking."

Another hesitation and then, "The weekend of the wedding. Mark was with someone."

"Who?"

He looked at her then, regret in his eyes. "What difference does—"

"*Who*?"

"Gina something. The sister of one of your bridesmaids."

She'd asked him to tell her. She wanted to know. But hearing the words sliced a fresh gash of pain through her heart, and she wished, desperately, that she had not asked. "You knew this then, and you never told me?"

"Addy. How could I?"

She stood, twisting her fingers together. "I thought you were different. That you would never lie to me. But you're not, are you?"

"I didn't think it was what you wanted to hear," he said, his voice low, appealing.

"Maybe not. But it was still the truth." She stood, opened the screen door and went inside without looking back.

CHAPTER THIRTEEN

AT FIRST GLANCE, the Mecklinberg Women's Correctional Facility could have been anything from a post office to a middle school. The truth became apparent, however, in the detail. The chain-link fence with rows of barbed wire strung across the top. The front gate where guards stood armed with rifles.

Culley hated coming here. Hated the feeling of bleakness that settled on him at the sight of it.

He'd left the house at just after five that morning. The four-hour drive gave him a good stretch of time to think about what had happened with Mark. Of how angry Addy was with him. He didn't blame her. He should have told her a long time ago.

He'd reached for the phone a dozen times before finally dialing the number. Claire had told him she was out in the orchard mowing. He'd left a message for her to call him back. But she hadn't. As he'd known she wouldn't.

She was angry with him. Maybe justifiably so.

All those years ago, he'd thought he was doing the right thing. Staying out of it. Not interfering.

He pulled into a parking space, cut the engine and sat there with his arms draped across the steering wheel. Had he been wrong not to tell her?

Mark had always been one of those guys who could justify his actions. One last fling before the wedding. And never again.

Over the years, Culley had questioned his decision. Maybe he should have told her. But it had felt like he would have been stepping into the middle of something for which his own motives could have been questioned.

And wasn't that the truth at the center of his decision to keep quiet?

He got out of the car and went inside the building. A stern-faced receptionist assessed him over the rim of coaster-size glasses. He told her why he was there.

Thirty minutes later, a guard led him to a small waiting room with two chairs and a skinny window that offered a glimpse at the outside world. The door opened, and Liz stepped into the room. The same guard from before closed the door and took his post on the other side.

"Hey," Liz said.

"Hey." Culley stared at her for a moment, a little shocked by the differences in her appearance since he last saw her.

She ran a hand across her hair, looking self-conscious. "I cut it."

As long as he had known her, Liz's hair had been her most notable feature. In college, other girls had tried to copy the effortless style of hers, but rarely pulled it off. "It looks nice."

She smiled. "Liar. I know it looks horrible. I don't know, I guess I really am hoping to start over. A new me."

"There's a lot of the old you that doesn't need changing," he said.

"Thanks. But we both know I've got a lot of work to do."

"Wanting to is the first step."

"I don't think it would be possible to want it more."

"Madeline said to say hello." He reached into his pocket and pulled out an envelope. "She asked me to give you this."

Liz held it for a moment, then slit open the back and pulled out a piece of red construction paper. She stared at it, a tear sliding down her cheek. She got up, went to the single window and looked out, longing in her expression. "I miss her so much.

But I would understand if you never wanted me to see her again."

"Liz—"

"From here, it seems like a dream. Like something that happened to someone else. When I think of what I did, of how many lives I've messed up, that I could have killed my child—" She broke off there, dropping her forehead onto one hand, a sob wrenching from her throat.

His heart in a knot, Culley crossed the room and put a hand on her back, feeling inadequate beyond words.

She turned, raising tear-filled eyes to his. "Sometimes I think I deserve to stay here for the rest of my life. And other times, I want out so badly I think I might die from it."

He pulled her to him, held her against him while she cried. All the old feelings of helplessness swamped him. "Liz. I believe in you. If you want to make another life for yourself, you will."

"Thank you," she said. "For coming here today. And for seeing hope in me. I'm sorry I threw away what we had. If I could do it over again—"

"Don't," he said. "Let's just think about the future, okay?"

She started to say something, then stopped. "Okay," she said.

ADDY STAYED BUSY on Tuesday, not giving herself time to think. She was in the warehouse late that morning, sorting through crates that needed to be repaired. Claire walked in with two bottles of water and handed her one. Peabody trailed in behind her, his tail straight in the air.

"Are you ready to talk about it?" Claire asked.

Addy put down her clipboard, took a sip of the cold water, then leaned over to brush her hand along Peabody's spine. He arched his back and offered a reluctant purr. "There's really nothing to talk about."

"You've been upset ever since Mark came here. I can see that."

She straightened and rubbed a thumb at the side of her temple. "How is it possible to be married to someone for eleven years and not know them?"

Claire sighed and sat down on an old wooden bench. "I think we know as much of a person as they want us to know."

"It's like there were two sides to him. I can't believe what a fool I was."

"You weren't a fool."

Addy sat down beside her, pressed her lips together, and then said, "I walked in on him with another woman. She was pregnant with his child."

"Oh, my dear." Claire reached out to put a hand on Addy's back.

"I married Mark thinking he was this faithful guy, that he would never—"

"Do what your father did?" Claire's expression wilted, and Addy could see that despite all the years that had passed, the pain was still there.

"We don't need to talk about that, Mama."

Claire set down her water bottle. "I think we do. I know we never did, and now I'm not sure why except that at first it was so painful. And then, well, I guess I felt like you blamed me."

Addy wished she could deny it. Amazing that it was only here, now, that she could see her father with new eyes. Realize that, like her mother, she had done nothing to cause her husband's infidelity. She looked down. "I'm so sorry, Mama."

Claire reached out and took her hand. "Don't be, honey. You felt as betrayed as I did."

"I blamed the wrong person though."

Peabody jumped up on the bench between them, rubbing his head against Claire's arm and then Addy's, as if trying to soothe them both.

"Sometimes when something beyond our understanding happens to us, we're so desperate to make sense of it that we lash out at whoever is closest." Claire smoothed a hand across her blue jeans, the knees long faded. "Ida was the one to tell me about your father's cheating. She saw him leaving a motel with the other woman one afternoon. She agonized for days before finally coming to me with it. And I didn't believe her. I accused her of being jealous because her own husband treated her so badly."

Addy stared at her mother, heard the knot of pain in her voice.

"It was an awful position for her to be in. She was trying to be loyal to me, and I threw it back in her face. I'm surprised she ever forgave me."

Addy looked down at her hands, guilt surging up. "I think I've just done the same thing to Culley. Mark was with someone on the weekend of our wedding, and Culley knew. But he never told me."

"Would you have believed him?"

"I honestly don't know. Maybe not."

Claire sighed. "Sometimes people do things for us because they care about us. But it's not always what we want to hear. Ida was being my friend. And maybe Culley thought he was being yours."

She reached out and placed her hand over Addy's. They sat that way for a long while, a new sense of understanding settling between them.

And Addy wondered if sometimes out of loss came the greatest gain.

IT TOOK A WEEK to sort through everything she was feeling. It was still almost impossible for her to believe that Mark could have been someone so different from the man she had thought him to be. But he had. And Culley wasn't to blame. Her mom was right. Maybe it had been easier to focus on what Culley had kept from her rather than the fact that Mark had been unfaithful from the beginning.

The one thing she knew was that she owed Culley an apology.

She drove over to his house around seven on Tuesday evening. Claire and Ida had gone to a movie together, so she was hoping he would be home. His Explorer was in the driveway, Madeline outside in the front yard, playing hopscotch.

Addy got out, raised a hand and waved.

Madeline ran over. "Hi, Addy."

Addy smiled. "How are you, Madeline?"

"Good. How's the deer?"

"She has quite an appetite."

"Can I come back and see her soon?"

"Anytime."

The front door opened, and Culley stepped out, his expression cautious. "Hey," he said.

She walked to the porch, stopping at the first step. She glanced down at the still-warm-from-the-oven plate in her hands. "It should have been humble pie, but I was hoping apple would do."

He looked at her for a long moment, then offered a half smile. "Apple works for me."

She handed him the plate.

"Smells good."

"It's Mama's apple-crisp recipe, but any deficiencies will be mine."

He beckoned her up the steps, calling out to Madeline that they would be in the kitchen. Inside, he set the pie plate on the table and said, "You okay?"

She nodded, not quite able to meet the concern in his eyes. She bit her lip, and then said, "I owe you an apology."

"You don't owe me anything, Addy."

"I do. I feel like such a fool. I guess the thought that you had known all along how clueless I was—"

"Addy, don't. It wasn't like that."

"Yeah. It was."

"I'm the one who's sorry," he said.

She looked up then, met his gaze. "See, that's the thing. You didn't do anything wrong."

He moved across the floor, stopping in front of her. "I've missed you," he said.

She looked up at him, considered making light of the confession, then opted for the truth. "I've missed you, too."

They watched each other for a few seconds, and Addy was glad, really glad, that she'd found the courage to come over here tonight.

The kiss was slow, easy, hello, I really *did* miss you. Her hands slid up around his neck, and he gathered her against him until it began to change direction, heating up fast.

"Daddy! Can you come here?"

Madeline's anxious voice rang out from the front yard. Culley dropped his forehead against Addy's, took a deep breath, and said, "Sorry. I'll be right back."

She smiled.

He left the kitchen and returned a few moments later. "Hopscotch emergency. Large brown spider on number seven. So where were we?"

"Headed toward trouble."

He grinned. "Oh, yeah, right."

Addy moved across the kitchen, out of reach. "So. Let's talk. What have you been doing?"

He blew out a sigh and ran a hand to the back of his neck. "Wondering how long I should wait before I came over to ask how I could make it up to you."

She got serious then. "There's nothing for you to make up."

"So why was Mark here?"

"He said he missed me. Which seems a little odd since he has a lover in her twenties and a baby boy to be a father to."

Culley's gaze widened. "Whew."

She shook her head. "I realized something about Mark. That he's always looking to someone else for happiness. And maybe he's going to have to find it in himself first."

Culley gave her a look of appreciation, then said in a low voice, "You've gotten a handle on this, haven't you?"

She lifted her shoulders. "I did a lot of thinking this week. I guess seeing Mark put me in a re-assessing mode. I've decided I'm not going back to D.C. I changed my leave of absence status to resignation."

Culley's eyes widened. "Wow. That's great. Really."

"I've been doing some research, had some ideas on how to make the orchard more of a niche business."

"I'm impressed."

"A lot of years of work have gone into it, mostly Mama's work. I don't want to see it go away."

He reached out, traced a finger along her jaw. "Neither do I."

The front door slapped open, and Madeline ran into the kitchen. "Was that apple pie?"

"It was," Addy said. "Would you like a piece?"

"Yes, please."

"Pull up a chair, honey," Culley said, opening a cabinet and reaching for three plates. He settled a warm smile on Addy, and in a voice intended for her ears only, said, "I'd like to see if a woman who looks this good can cook."

"THAT PIE WAS OUTSTANDING."

"Just outstanding?" Addy teased.

"Scale of one-to-ten, nine-point-eight," Culley said.

"Very smart. If you'd said ten, naturally I wouldn't have believed you."

"Naturally."

"So what was the two-tenths deduction for?"

"Not getting to kiss you after you'd had a bite."

"I can live with that, I guess."

They were sitting outside on lounge chairs with thick cushions. Culley had laid a stone terrace in the backyard at some point, and it made a nice centerpiece for the boundary of beech trees that circled out from the house. The evening air had cooled, the humidity dipping enough to make the temperature pleasant.

They were quiet for a while, and Addy sensed he was preoccupied. "Is something wrong?" she asked.

He leaned back against the chair, hands above his head. "I went to see Liz last week."

Addy heard a new tightness in his voice. "And?"

"I think she wants to do the right thing this time."

"What are her plans?"

"I don't know. She said she was still working on her road map."

"Will she come here?"

"I didn't ask her to." He sighed. "Is that horrible?"

Addy considered her words. "You've found a way to go on. Madeline has needed that. Seeing Liz must feel like opening the door to all the painful stuff again."

"I worry about Madeline. How this will affect her."

"She'll be okay," Addy said, reaching out and lacing her fingers through his.

"I have to go to Richmond tomorrow for a couple of days. I leave in the morning. The Summer

Festival's in town this weekend. I had planned to take Madeline. Will you go with us?"

Addy smiled. "I'd love to."

"Great." He looked at her for a long moment, and then, "I don't know what's going to happen with Liz. But if the road gets bumpy for a while, will you hang on?"

"I'm not going anywhere," she said.

He leaned in and kissed her in a way that said things words couldn't. He stood, pulled her to her feet and deepened the kiss. And there under the promise of a full moon, she kissed him back.

CHAPTER FOURTEEN

THE REST OF the week passed in slow motion. Culley called each night, and they talked on the phone like two teenagers who never ran out of things to say.

And she loved the way it felt. This man she had once known as a boy, as a friend, became more important to her every day.

There had been a point, not so long ago, when her self-image had been flattened to a single dimension by the choices Mark had made.

But she had come to realize that those choices were about him and *his* shortcomings. Not hers. And she had Culley to thank for helping her see that.

It was a very good place to be.

For the remainder of the week, Addy worked nonstop on a proposal for the orchard. Through the Internet, she had found a tremendous amount of information on organic farming. The more she read, the more excited she became about the possibilities.

Over breakfast on Thursday morning, she laid the notebook she had compiled in front of Claire and said, "I think we can make this work."

Claire opened the cover and flipped through some of the pages. "Organic?"

Addy nodded. "You were right. Competing with the big guys isn't going to be possible for us. By converting our methods to organic, we could position ourselves in a niche market of specialty grocery stores and restaurants. I think we could find a large market in D.C. alone, and that's only four hours from here."

Claire flipped through the remainder of the notebook without saying anything. "Addy, you're a lawyer. And a good one. Are you sure you want to give that up? Because there aren't any guarantees here."

"No. But if I've learned anything this past year, it's that there aren't any guarantees anywhere. So we might as well try the roads that feel like they have something to offer."

"What if it doesn't work?" Claire asked.

"Then we will have tried. And I'll be satisfied with that." Addy hesitated, searching for words. "I'm glad I came back, Mama. That we've had this time together. That I understand some things I didn't understand before."

Claire got up from her chair and hugged Addy. "Whether we're successful with this venture or not, you will never know what it means to me that you want to try."

"Thank you, Mama."

"I'm the one who should be thanking you." She turned to leave the room, then swung back. "I forgot to tell you. Culley called this morning and said he would be late getting back tomorrow. He was supposed to take Madeline shopping for a dance recital dress and wondered if you would want to take her."

"I'd love to," Addy said.

"Ida has all the details."

"I'll give her a call."

ADDY PICKED MADELINE up from school at just after three Friday afternoon. The little girl got in the car, a shy smile on her face.

"Okay," Addy said, pulling out of the parking lot, "we're on a mission. I know of three stores that carry great clothes for your age. What do you say we hit them all?"

Madeline nodded with quiet enthusiasm. "Do you think they might have something in blue?"

"Is that your favorite color?"

"Yes."

Addy smiled. "Then we'll definitely have to find something in blue."

They drove into Roanoke, stopped at the first store where, according to Madeline, the dresses had too much frill and lace. In the second store, they found one she really liked, but not in her size. It was in the third store, a quaint boutique-size shop called Puddles, where they found what she was looking for. She came out of the dressing room, a pleased smile at the corners of her mouth.

"Oh, Madeline, you look so pretty," Addy said.

The dress was a Catimini, a French brand of adorable children's clothes. Sleeveless, it was royal blue with skinny kiwi-colored stripes running through it.

Madeline stood in front of the mirror, smoothing a hand over the waist of the dress. "Does it look all right?"

"Better than all right." Addy smiled. "It's perfect for you. You'll be the prettiest girl at the dance."

In the mirror, Madeline's eyes were uncertain. "Do you think Daddy will like it?"

"I think he'll love it," she said.

Madeline smiled. "Okay."

They bought the dress and a pair of strappy white sandals to go with it. On the way home, they stopped for a sandwich at a small diner just short of the Franklin County line. The place was busy, and they were given the last table for two in a back corner by the window. The waitress came and took their drink orders, returning a couple of minutes later with Addy's iced tea and Madeline's milk.

Madeline took a sip, then stared out the window. "You know about my mom?"

Addy emptied a pack of sugar in her tea, stirred it with a long spoon, the ice clinking against the edges of the glass. "Yeah," she said.

"Pretty awful, huh?"

Addy nodded.

Madeline fiddled with her straw, bit her lower lip, and then said, "I wasn't very good that day. Mama said I was driving her crazy. I saw her get the bottle out of the closet where she kept it hid. She didn't think I knew about it, but I'd seen her get it before. Maybe if I'd been better that day, she wouldn't have done that. And maybe none of it would have happened. Maybe she wouldn't be in prison."

"Oh, Madeline. That's a huge burden for a little girl to be carrying around. And you know, that's the thing I never realized until I got to be a grown-up. When I was twelve, my daddy left. He just went away one day and never came back. I couldn't even begin to understand why. I thought I could say something, do something that would make him change his mind. Be better, look better, blame my mom. What I didn't understand then was that he made that decision all by himself. And it wasn't because of anything that I did or my mama did. People don't always do the right things. But children aren't supposed to feel bad for the decisions that grown-ups make. It's hard not to because sometimes it's not easy to make sense of the things that happen. But you were just a little girl. And still are." She reached across and put her hand on top of Madeline's. "You weren't responsible for what happened."

Madeline looked up at her, her eyes darkened with what looked like relief. "Thank you," she said.

THEY ATE GRILLED cheese sandwiches and homemade peach cobbler topped with vanilla ice cream for dessert.

On the way out to the parking lot, Madeline thanked Addy for the meal. "It was really nice of you to take me today."

"It was my pleasure," Addy said. "What's more fun than shopping for clothes when they look as great on you as that dress did?"

Madeline beamed, and something squeezed at

Addy's heart, a connection forming between the
two of them that felt like an unexpected gift.

She hit the remote, and they got in the car. Addy
backed out of the parking space.

"Addy, look!" Madeline pointed at the trio of
green Dumpsters separated from the restaurant by
a tall wooden fence.

"What is it?"

"A puppy. He went behind the middle Dumpster."

Addy pulled back into the space and cut the engine. "Let's go see."

They walked to the back of the Dumpsters.
Huddled beside one of the big containers was a
dog about the size of a half gallon of milk. He was
solid black with a thin strip of white down his
chest. His ribs stuck out, and he was holding one
paw off the ground as if he'd injured it.

Addy dropped to the ground beside the puppy,
held out a hand. "Hey, little fella."

The puppy shrank from her, leaning against the
Dumpster as if it might somehow absorb him.

"Do you think he's lost?" Madeline asked.

"Someone probably dropped him here."

"Why?"

Addy sighed. "Because sometimes people don't
live up to their responsibilities."

"You mean like finding a home for him?"

Addy nodded. "I think I have some crackers in the console of the car. Would you get them for me?"

Madeline bounded off and was back in a few seconds. "Here you go."

"Thank you. Let's see what kind of an impression these make on him." Addy opened the pack and placed one in front of the puppy. He gave her a wary look, leaned closer to sniff, then gobbled it up in one bite.

"He likes it," Madeline said, delight in her voice.

Addy gave him another which disappeared with like speed. By the third cracker, he was sniffing out of Addy's hand and wagging his tail. Addy lifted his right paw. "Ooh. He's got a nasty cut on one of his pads. That must really hurt."

Madeline leaned in for a closer look, made a sound of sympathy. "What should we do?" she asked.

Addy leaned over and scooped him up. "We can't leave him here," she said. "Looks like we're going home with a puppy."

Madeline's eyes went wide, her smile one of delight. "Really?"

"Really," Addy said and smiled back.

SHE CALLED CULLEY from the car phone. He'd just gotten home. She told him what had happened.

"And let me guess," he said, his voice warm, teasing. "You're on your way to Doc Nolen's."

"He's not in great shape."

"Anything I can do?"

"No. But is it okay if I'm a bit late with Madeline?"

"Sure. I'll see you when you get here."

"Okay."

"Hey, want me to call Doc and tell him you're coming?"

"That would be great."

"Done."

They arrived at the clinic in less than twenty minutes. Madeline had spent the duration of the drive throwing yearning glances over the seat at the puppy who had curled up in a ball and fallen asleep.

"He looks so tired," she said.

"I'm sure he is. He's too young to be fending for himself."

Addy lifted him out of the back seat, and they walked across the parking lot. Doc stood at the front door of the clinic, shaking his head.

"I see you've recruited the youngest Rutherford," he said.

"Actually, Madeline is the one who saw him."

"That so?" Doc asked the young girl.

She nodded.

"I expect he couldn't have hoped for anybody better to come along. You taking him home with you?"

Madeline looked at Addy. "I don't know."

"We wanted to see if you could check him out. He has a hurt paw for one thing."

"Let's take a look," Doc said, directing them inside.

Thirty minutes later, he declared them all set. "Change the dressing on the paw twice a day and apply that ointment I gave you. Other than a few ear mites, he's good to go. Bring him back in a month or so for the rest of his shots."

"Thank you, Doc."

"Don't mention it. I see way too many thrown away animals. I wish they all could be as lucky as this guy. Tell Claire I said hello."

"I will."

Madeline sat in the back with the puppy once they left the clinic. Addy glanced in the rearview mirror and saw her rubbing its small head with adoration on her face.

Culley met them when they pulled up in front of the house.

Addy opened the back door. Madeline slid out, the sleepy puppy in her arms. "Look, Daddy!" she said. "Isn't he perfect?"

He touched the puppy's nose. "Pretty darn cute." He looked at Addy and smiled. "So the shopping trip turned into a little something extra?"

"A little," she said, smiling.

"Bring him inside."

Madeline carried him in. Culley had already arranged a big pillow on the floor with a water bowl. "I've got some chicken in the fridge. No bones. That be okay to give him?"

"Thank you," Addy said. "That would be great."

Culley got the chicken, and they all three sat on the floor, watching, while the puppy made short work of it.

"So who's keeping him?" Culley asked.

Addy looked at Madeline. "That's up to you two."

Madeline kept her gaze on the puppy, rubbing his tummy. He rolled over on his back, stuck his feet in the air.

Culley put a hand on Madeline's shoulder. "What do you think, honey?"

"I can't keep him," Madeline said in a low voice.

"We've got plenty of room—"

Madeline jumped up from the floor, her lower lip trembling. "No," she said. "I can't keep him. I just can't." She ran from the room and tore up the stairs.

Addy looked at Culley, her heart in her throat. "I'm sorry."

Culley stood. "Let me go talk to her. Can you wait a few minutes?"

"Sure."

He nodded and headed upstairs.

CULLEY KNOCKED AT his daughter's door, then turned the knob and stepped into the room. She was huddled in a ball on her bed, oversize pink pillows cast aside, a stuffed bunny tucked under her arm.

He sat on the edge of the mattress and smoothed a hand over her hair. "What is it, baby? What's wrong?"

She shook her head, bit her lip.

"You want the puppy, don't you?"

Silence, and then a sober nod.

"Then why didn't you take him?"

A minute or more passed before she sat up against the pillows, her eyes focused on her lap. "Because if I love him, something bad will happen to him."

It took a moment for Culley to absorb the words, but when they finally settled, their weight left a crack in his heart. He lifted her hand, clasped it between his own. "Why would you say that, honey?"

She shook her head again.

He had asked, but he already knew the answer. It stirred an old and futile anger inside him. "Baby, what happened to your mom wasn't your fault. It wasn't."

She looked up at him, anguish clear in her eyes, the sharpness of it shocking. He'd let himself believe she'd reached a more peaceful place in accepting what had happened to Liz. He'd been deluding himself. He gathered her up in his arms, held her tight against him. He started to speak, but the words stuck in his throat, and he swallowed hard. "Listen to me, okay? Sometimes grown-ups make choices that end up being a mistake. That's what your mom did. And you had nothing to do with it. Nothing. Do you understand that?"

Madeline nodded against his chest, tears soaking through his shirt.

He sat back, looked down at her. "I love you, sweetie. I'll be right back, okay?"

She nodded and wiped her eyes with the back of her hand.

Downstairs, he found Addy sitting on the couch with the puppy.

"Is she all right?" she asked.

He ran a hand through his hair. "I think she will be. Because of what happened to Liz, she's convinced herself that something bad will happen to anything she loves."

"Oh, Culley. She wanted the puppy then?"

"Yeah." He paused. "Come with me."

"Are you sure?"

"Very."

IT WAS ALMOST ten o'clock when Culley walked Addy out to her car.

"Thank you," he said, his hands shoved inside the pockets of his jeans.

"I didn't do anything."

"Yes, you did," he said. "Madeline had a great time today. She looked happier tonight than I've seen her in a long time."

"We did talk a little. I think she blames herself for the accident. She said she hadn't been very good that day, and that was why her mom drank."

Culley swallowed hard, shook his head.

"I talked to her about how children aren't responsible for adults' decisions. I hope that was okay."

"I should have figured that out. That's what she's been holding on to all this time."

"She's a wonderful child, Culley."

"She is," he said. "And I think Hershey will be good for her. She needs a buddy."

"I'm glad. And I like the name."

Culley leaned back against the car then, looped his arms around her waist and pulled her to him. "I keep getting hit with this same feeling."

"What's that?"

"That this is somehow all meant to be. Our place in each other's lives."

She pressed her cheek to his chest, listened to the steady beat of his heart. And thought that's what he'd given her, a regrounding, a steadiness that made her look at what lay ahead with a new kind of hopefulness. "That's a nice thought," she said.

He tipped her face up and kissed her, a thorough, sweeping kiss that neither of them was eager to end.

The front porch door slapped open. Madeline called out, "I think Hershey needs to go outside."

Addy smiled. "Okay, I'm going," she said and then, "Good night, Madeline. 'Night, Hershey."

"Good night, Addy," Madeline said.

Culley leaned close to her ear. "More later?"

"More later," she said and smiled.

CHAPTER FIFTEEN

ON SATURDAY MORNING, Addy was up with the daylight after a night of fitful sleep. Culley was picking her up at eleven. She was dressed and ready at ten-thirty, after another round of changing outfits. Claire left around ten to do some errands, after which she was going on to the festival to work in one of the food booths for Harper's Mill Baptist.

Addy was sitting on the front step when Culley pulled into the driveway. He got out, walked straight over and said, "Could we go inside for just a minute?"

She blinked, then glanced at the Explorer where Madeline sat in the back seat, a cell phone to her ear.

"She's talking to Grandma. I told her we'd be right out."

Addy climbed the steps and opened the door. He followed her in. "Is everything all right?" she asked, turning around.

He stepped forward and pulled her to him, kissing her the way a man kisses a woman he has missed. Addy let that register, wrapped her arms around his neck and kissed him back with the same kind of honesty.

"You cannot imagine how much I wanted to do that," he said.

"I know how much I wanted you to."

"See, we are compatible."

Addy looked up at him, smiling. "It would be hard to argue against this part of it."

The look in his eyes made Addy feel wanted, needed. He dipped his head and kissed her again.

"I could really get used to this," she said.

"I'm hoping you will."

"Okay." Deep breath. "Madeline is waiting. We're going to get in trouble if we don't get out there."

"I'm already in trouble," he said.

She smiled, took his hand and led him back outside. Madeline had rolled down her window, calling out, "Hi, Addy."

"How's Hershey?"

"Good. I wanted to bring him, but since he's so little, we thought he might get too tired. Could I see the deer before we go?"

"Absolutely," Addy said. "You won't believe how she's grown."

They walked to the barn. Addy opened the stall door, and Madeline slipped inside, dropping onto her knees. The deer walked over to sniff her hand.

"I've been giving her apples every evening," Addy said. "She loves them."

"Are you going to keep her forever?" Madeline asked.

"She's not really mine," Addy said. "When she's ready, I'll have to let her go."

Madeline nodded, rubbing the deer's head.

"We'd better go, honey," Culley said.

"Okay." Madeline got up, gave the deer a last lingering look and walked out of the stall.

THE HARPER'S MILL Summer Festival was held every July.

It was unusual weather for this time of year in Virginia, the air without humidity, the sky a blinding blue. A perfect day, really.

From Addy's point of view, it was perfect from all other angles as well. The three of them started at one end of the fairgrounds and worked their way through two dozen rides, a Ferris wheel, a spider wheel, carousel horses, bumper cars. The bumper cars were the best. Addy couldn't remember the last time she'd laughed so much. She and

Madeline shared a car and bumped Culley so often that he finally faked a problem and then shot off to the other side of the arena when they let up for a moment.

"So admit it," Addy teased as they headed to the Ferris wheel for one last ride before lunch. "Women are better drivers."

"Women are without mercy," he said, smiling. "I think there was a little repressed road rage in there somewhere."

She laughed. "It's the D.C. driving."

Culley rode the Ferris wheel with Madeline while Addy went in search of Claire and Ida, whom they were meeting for lunch. She found them both at the Harper's Mill Baptist booth, and they all walked back to meet Culley and Madeline.

They found a picnic table in the shade, weighed it down with a ridiculous amount of food, filling themselves on fresh-squeezed lemonade and hot dogs, topping it off with a big poof of cotton candy.

"I wish we got to eat this every day, Daddy," Madeline said.

"This will be your sugar quota until Christmas."

"Daddy!"

"Well, Halloween, anyway."

"Look, that clown has balloons!" Madeline jumped up from the table. "Could we get one?"

"He looks like he's having a slow day, doesn't he?" He put a hand on Addy's shoulder, gave it a squeeze. "Be right back."

"Take your time," she said, with a smile.

The two of them trotted off after the clown. Claire went to the rest room, saying she would be right back, leaving Addy and Ida alone at the table.

"Madeline had a great time with you yesterday," Ida said.

"It was fun. We came home with a bit more than we planned to," she said, smiling.

"I heard all about the puppy. Exactly what she needs. I've worried about her for a long time. She carried around a lot of guilt that had no place on her little shoulders."

"It was a lot to accept," Addy said softly.

"Yes, it was."

Claire returned to the table, rubbing her eye.

"Are you all right?" Addy asked.

"I've torn a contact. That's what I get for trying to be modern."

"Do you have your glasses with you?"

"I have a pair in the car."

"I'll get them for you," Addy said.

"I can go, honey."

"I don't mind," she insisted. "Where are they?"

"In the glove compartment." Claire handed her the keys. "I parked over by the side entrance."

"Okay. Be right back."

THE CLOWN WAS a good salesman, and Culley arrived back at the table with a balloon for Addy, Claire and his mom as well. They said Addy had gone to the car to get Claire's glasses. He asked them to watch Madeline for a while and went after her. As much fun as they'd had, they hadn't had a minute alone all morning, and he itched to pick up where they'd left off earlier.

Halfway through the parking lot, he heard a scream. Addy. A knife of adrenaline sliced through him. He took off at a dead run, winding through parked cars until he spotted her. A tall man with a ponytail had her backed against the door of Claire's car.

"Hey!" Culley yelled.

The man looked over his shoulder, jabbed a finger at Addy's chest, said something Culley couldn't hear, then took off.

Culley stopped in front of Addy, a hand on each of her shoulders. "Are you all right?"

She nodded, obviously shaken.

"I'm going after him."

"Culley, wait—"

But he was already running, weaving through cars and people who turned to stare. The man reached the edge of the lot, glanced over his shoulder and broke into a sprint. Culley hit the last row of cars and opened up his stride.

The man headed down the two-lane road that served as the entrance to the fairgrounds, both of them in a dead run. Culley gained on him, and then the guy held his own for a few moments. He looked over his shoulder again, hit an uneven spot of ground and toppled. Culley crashed to a stop and jumped the guy.

He threw a punch, missing Culley's jaw by a fraction of an inch. Culley threw one back, connected with bone, his own knuckles screaming.

The guy howled about his ankle. "I think it's broken."

"Who are you?" Culley shouted, pinning the man's shoulders to the ground.

"None of your damn business."

Culley punched him again.

The guy shook his head like a dog getting rid of water after a swim.

"I'll ask again. Who are you?"

"Man, my ankle's killing me."

"Then you'd better tell me fast."

"I work for Dudley Contracting."

"Raymond Dudley?"

"One and the same." This with sarcasm.

"And what's his interest in this?"

"Why don't you ask him?"

"I'm asking you."

The man glared at him. "He wants the interstate to go through the county. He paid me to persuade the dissenters."

"So you're issuing threats to two women who are trying to hold on to a place they love?"

He clamped a hand to his jaw. "They might as well give up. They're not going to win against Dudley and Powers."

"Congressman Powers?"

"That would be the one."

Culley got up before giving in to the urge to punch him again.

"Culley!"

He turned just as Addy ran up. "I called the sheriff from my cell phone," she said. "Are you okay?"

Culley dropped his hands to his knees, sucked in a few breaths. "I'm fine. Are you?"

"Yes." She looked at the man who lay groaning on the ground beside them.

"I don't think you'll have to worry about any more rocks through your window."

A siren whistled through the air, and then two brown county cars roared up. The sheriff and two deputies got out.

Sheriff Ramsey looked at Culley. "What's going on?"

Culley threw a glance at the man on the ground. "I believe he'll tell you everything."

CLAIRE AND IDA were both shaken to hear what had happened.

Culley had a call he wanted to make, and while he stood a short distance away talking on his cell phone, Addy gave them what details the sheriff had managed to pry out of the man before hauling him off to the county jail.

Claire frowned. "Raymond Dudley's one of Congressman Powers biggest supporters."

Culley returned to the table, putting his phone in his pocket. "And Dudley Contracting is the candidate for the hauling work if the interstate goes through Harper's Mill," he said.

"That's interesting," Addy said.

"Yeah, I just called a friend of mine at the paper and suggested he might want to explore the connection."

Claire sat down on the picnic table bench, one hand to her chest. "He could have hurt you, Addy."

"I think his intent was more to scare me. But it doesn't matter now. It's over."

Claire hugged her, holding on extratight.

Culley and Addy salvaged the day for Madeline's sake, spending the next few hours letting her choose whatever she wanted to do. She ran out of gas around four o'clock, falling asleep in Culley's arms, her head on his shoulder.

They traced their steps back to the booth where Claire and Ida were working.

Madeline revived long enough to lift her head and say, "Do I still get to spend the night with Grandma?"

"You're awfully pooped," Culley said. "Sure you don't want to go home?"

"Grandma rented a movie, and she said Hershey could come."

"Hard to argue with that."

Madeline issued a sleepy nod.

"Okay, then."

"You two go find something to do," Ida said. "We'll be fine. Claire, maybe you'd like to join us?"

"Actually, I have a date tonight."

Addy glanced up, surprised.

"I know," Claire said, smiling. "Shocking, huh?"

"Well, no," Addy said. "Not shocking. Doc Nolen, right?"

Claire nodded. "He stopped by the booth a while ago and asked if I'd like to go to dinner."

Addy noted the color in her mother's cheeks, the thread of excitement in her voice. "Does he know about Peabody?"

"No, but that would be a good litmus test, wouldn't it?"

Addy smiled. "It certainly would."

Claire smiled back. "Don't worry about the deer. I'll feed her before I go."

"Are you sure?"

"Positive."

Addy kissed her cheek and said, "Thank you. Have fun."

CULLEY OFFERED TO cook dinner for Addy under the stipulation that she not hold his less than superior culinary skills against him.

They arrived at his house just after five-thirty. Ida and Madeline came by and picked up Hershey who ran circles in the yard, before settling into the car with his head on Madeline's lap.

Once they'd left, Culley offered Addy the use of his shower. She took him up on it, feeling as if she had a thin layer of dust coated to her skin. She stood under the warm spray, trying not to think about the fact that he stood in this same shower every day. Or what it would be like to have him in here with her. Time to get out. There was trouble in that line of thinking.

She got dressed and went back downstairs to find him in the kitchen pulling things out of the refrigerator.

He looked up, smiled at her. "I have a limited repertoire, but I make a notable chopped salad."

"Sounds perfect. How can I help?"

"You handy with a knife?"

"Fairly."

He passed her a cutting board that had cucumbers and an assortment of bell peppers on it.

"Would you like some wine or something? I could probably find a bottle somewhere."

"No," she said. "Better not. My track record's questionable."

He grinned. "Playing it safe, huh?"

"Yeah," she said, smiling back.

The kitchen had a lived-in, comfortable feel to it. And Culley obviously knew his way around. It surprised her somehow. Mark wouldn't have been able to locate a broiling pan with a compass.

Culley had put on some music, John Mayer, and it drifted down from the ceiling speakers.

"Did I thank you for saving me today?"

"No thanks necessary."

"Plenty necessary. Thank you," she said.

"You're welcome."

Their gazes held for a moment, something warm and beckoning in the wordless exchange.

Addy looked away first. "So do you think there's a connection between Dudley and Powers?" she asked.

"I don't know, but they've definitely been the two strongest voices for pushing the interstate through Harper's Mill. And now it turns out Dudley's been behind all these threats people have been getting. It'll be interesting to see what comes out in the wash."

They worked on the salad, chopping and dicing. Addy thought it amazing that the two of them could enjoy something as simple and mundane as making dinner, but it was the act of doing it together that made it enjoyable. "This is nice," she said.

"What?"

"Just being here. Doing this." She hesitated. "Mark and I never did this kind of thing."

"Yeah?"

She lifted a shoulder. "For a long time, we were both consumed with the career thing. Getting ahead. I was as guilty as he was. But somewhere along the way, it started to feel like there should be more. That it wasn't enough."

"Did you want children?"

She nodded.

"And Mark didn't?"

"He said he wasn't ready. I guess in the end what he meant was he wasn't ready with me."

Culley put down his knife, turned her to him, looked into her eyes. "I don't know what was going on with Mark. But I do know this. He was an incredibly lucky man. And I think he's only just now figured that out."

She looked down, shook her head. "It doesn't matter."

He tipped her chin up with one finger. "It matters."

"Thank you."

He leaned in and kissed her then. And it felt so right and natural, as if this was where she belonged, like a place she'd been trying to find for a very long time, now recognized.

She put down her own knife, slipped her arms around his neck, and they kissed some more, a man and woman enjoying one another. "Back to You" was the current song, and the lyrics somehow fit the moment, conjured a longing in her for past and present, some mingling of the two.

After a few minutes, they went back to work, cutting, slicing, knocking elbows and bumping knuckles when they reached for the same vegetable.

"A masterpiece," Culley declared when they were done.

"Too pretty to eat," she agreed.

They sat outside on the stone terrace, talking about anything and everything.

Something about the night felt rare and special. They shared a few lingering looks that made words unnecessary. Addy found herself wishing she could stretch it out, make it last.

When they were done, they took their plates inside and cleaned up the kitchen. She turned on the dishwasher, wiped down the counter while he put everything away.

"Okay," he said, taking her hand. "I've got something to show you."

"What?" She smiled, following him into the living room, warmth emanating up from their entwined fingers.

He left her in the center of the floor. "Be right back."

He disappeared for a few moments, and then was back with two big photo albums which he held up and said, "How brave are you?"

She made a face and said, "How far back do they go?"

"Far enough."

She tipped her head. "All right. Let's see how bad it is."

They sat cross-legged in the middle of the rug, her right knee touching his left. He placed an album on the floor in front of them, opened the cover.

School pictures covered the first few pages, first grade up. Culley with bangs cut straight across his forehead. Addy with a gap-toothed smile. In one picture, Culley's shirt was buttoned all the way to his throat. And there was one of Addy wearing a pointy-collared dress, one side of which was wet from where she'd had a habit of sucking on it.

"Oh, my gosh," Addy said, clamping a hand to her mouth.

There were shots of the two of them at nine and ten, when they'd spent most of their summers riding around bareback on ponies and swimming in the orchard pond.

"Our sense of fashion was amazing," Addy said, laughing. "You actually wore parachute pants!"

"And how'd you get your hair that big?" he asked, pointing at one photo taken after Addy had begged her mom to take her to the beauty shop for a perm.

Into the second album, Mark began to appear in the pictures. There was one of the three of them at the Cliffs, a wall of rock at nearby Smith Mountain Lake where they used to go in the summertime and dive from the top into the deep, cool water below.

In the first few pictures, the three of them were side by side, most of the time with Addy in the middle, arms locked around one another. But then the poses changed, and Addy and Mark stood together with Culley off to the side.

Addy looked up and found Culley's gaze on her.

"I thought he was the luckiest guy in the world," he said, the look in his eyes suddenly serious.

The words touched something still tender inside her. She thumbed through the remainder of the album more quickly, closing the cover just as the clock in the foyer struck nine. She sat back with her palms on the floor behind her. "Painful, but fun. Thank you."

He set the albums on the coffee table next to them, anchored an elbow on either thigh and brushed his hand across the rug. "For the record, if I could do it over again, I would have given Mark a run for his money."

Addy looked at him, something inside her flipping over. "What does that mean?"

He drew in a deep breath, looked as if he were considering what he was about to say, and then said, "That I had feelings for you that went beyond friendship, but I didn't have the courage to act on them. You were crazy about him. And I was, you know, the guy you grew up with."

She propped an elbow on one knee, rested her cheek on a balled up fist. "Why is it that we can be so sure we're right about what we feel, and yet we get down the road to look back and wonder what we were thinking?"

"I don't know, but maybe sometimes we get shaped into a better version of ourselves by those choices. At least, if we're lucky."

Addy considered the words. "That morning when I got my eyes opened about Mark, it was like I began to see everything else for what it was as well. That I was accepting a life without children, keeping my nose to the grindstone at work so I didn't have to think about the holes in my personal life."

"Maybe we're willing to settle sometimes, just because it's easier than making a change. And you know what I realize now?"

"What?"

"Those moments we let go by. The ones where we wish we'd said what we wanted to say, did what we wanted to do. Most of the time you never get them back. I knew how I felt about you all those years ago, and I didn't take the chance and tell you." He looked at her for a long moment. "So I'm telling you now. You were amazing to me then. And you still are."

Emotion rose up from somewhere deep inside, preventing her from speaking. She looked into his eyes, let him see how the words had touched her.

The song on the CD changed. Something about missed chances and the second time around. And it was in that moment that Addy realized she had two choices. She could let what had happened with Mark leave a hole inside her into which every good thing that came into her life would eventually fall. Or, she could choose to see what had happened as an opportunity to, as Culley had said, be a better version of herself.

Life didn't come with any guarantees. Reaching out for something you wanted always meant there was the possibility you might later lose it.

But to never reach out meant you would never know.

She leaned forward, touched her lips to his, kissed him softly. He kissed her back, tentative, testing kisses, like the first steps of a new dance. They moved carefully at first, finding the rhythm, each step imbuing them with increasing confidence, stripping away the barriers of caution.

Addy could have kissed him forever, just like this, as if they had all the time in the world, as if it were too good not to savor. Everything about this night felt different to Addy. *She* felt different. As if she were here in the arms of a man to whom she was drawn in a wealth of ways. The past and who they had been to one another now layered with the present, the people they were discovering more each day. She liked who he was, this man he had become.

Another song slipped by, and then another. The kissing changed tone, his hands slipped up the back of her shirt, splayed at her waist.

They changed angles, and he pulled her across his lap, sideways at first, and they kissed like that for a good while. And then he put his hands on her hips, turned her so that they were sitting belly to belly, her legs on either side of him. All along, still kissing, feelings jolting to life beneath the exploration of their hands. She ran her palms across his wide shoulders, and then down his back, fitting closer even as it seemed they couldn't get close enough.

He pulled back, hands at the bottom of her shirt. "Is this okay?"

With her eyes, she gave him permission, and he lifted her shirt over her head, tossing it on the floor beside them. She undid his buttons, one at a time, then slid his shirt from his shoulders. Admired him for a few moments, then wrapped her arms around his neck, and they got close again. She felt an overwhelming rush of gladness to be here, to be with him. And for the fact that unlike that night in New York, this had something different at its center. Something that stood on its own, without the weight of the baggage she had been carrying around then.

He reached over, pulled a couple of pillows off the couch, and they stretched out on the thick Oriental rug. She lay on her back, and he lay half across her, one leg in between hers.

They kissed some more, taking their time.

He raised up on one elbow, sent a long look down the length of her.

She gave him an uncertain smile. "What?"

"I could just sit and look at you."

Her face went warm. "You're too good at this."

"That was no line, Addy. I don't have any reason to say anything I don't mean."

She put a hand on his arm. "I'm sorry. I didn't mean it like that."

He leaned down, kissed her again.

"Are we making out?" she asked.

"Yeah, I think so."

"I forgot it could be this much fun."

"Me, too."

They kissed some more. Switched places, and now she was on top, his hands on the back of her thighs, urging her closer.

He pulled back, stopped kissing her. "Addy."

"Umm?"

"If this is all we do, it's okay by me."

She tucked her hair behind her ear, dropped to the floor beside him, rested her cheek on his chest. "Was it something I said?"

He smoothed a hand over her hair, kissed the top of her head. "I don't want to do anything you're not ready to do. What's going on between us is too important to rush. If you're not ready—"

She raised up, touched a finger to his lips. "Thank you. Not just for saying it. For meaning it."

He got to his feet and pulled her up beside him, arms around her waist. He ducked his head and kissed her, then took her hand and led her to the stairs. They walked up side by side, stopping at the door of his room where they stood for a few moments, looking at one another.

"You're sure?"

"I'm sure," she said.

He lifted her up in his arms, shouldered the door open and stepped into the room. He dipped down, gave her a long thorough kiss, then kicked the door closed behind them.

CHAPTER SIXTEEN

ADDY STRETCHED, arching her back. "How is that possible?"

Culley raised up on one elbow and traced a finger down the length of her arm. "What?"

"That it could be better each time."

"The response a man lives for."

"Like you haven't heard it before."

He dropped back onto a pillow, stared up at the ceiling. "You have this lady-killer image of me that's not entirely accurate. Pretty far from it, actually."

"And you mind?"

"I'm just afraid I might have to live up to it one day."

She put a hand on his chest. "I guess it always intimidated me."

"What?"

"How crazy girls were about you."

He looked at her for a few seconds. "It's no big deal when it's not the right girl."

She leaned over, kissed him. His arms slipped around her waist to pull her across him.

"It's after midnight," she said.

"Very late," he agreed.

"I should get home."

"Stay a little longer?" This with a kiss on her neck, a hand at the small of her back.

She smiled. "I find it really hard to say no to you."

He smoothed her hair back from her face, rubbed a thumb across her cheekbone. "That's because you're the right girl."

She stayed a little longer.

IT WAS NEARLY 2:00 a.m. when they drove up the orchard road and stopped in front of the house.

They'd been quiet most of the drive over, but it was a comfortable, satisfied kind of quiet. There were a lot of questions between them, but Addy felt no sense of urgency for answers. And maybe that was what felt so right about what was happening. The fact that it was revealing itself at a pace of its own.

"Claire's not going to ground you, is she?"

Addy smiled. "She might if she sees what time it is."

He smiled back, and then with a more serious expression said, "I had a great time tonight."

"So did I."

"Can I just make sure we're clear on something?"

She nodded.

"That wasn't a casual thing for me."

"For me, either."

"I don't want to rush you, put pressure on you—"

"You're not," she said, reaching out to touch his arm. "It was a perfect night. Really."

"Okay," he said.

"Okay."

"I'll call you."

She opened her door, got out. "Good night."

"'Night."

She closed the door, walked halfway to the front porch, then turned and watched until the taillights of the Explorer disappeared into the dark.

CLAIRE HAD BREAKFAST ready the next morning when Addy came downstairs.

"That smells great," she said.

"I made a batch of blueberry muffins. They'll be out of the oven in a few minutes. Coffee's ready."

"Thanks." Addy poured herself a cup, then looked up to find Claire studying her.

"You look happy," she said.

Addy took a sip of her coffee, aimed her expression at neutral. "I am. It's kind of terrifying."

Claire opened the oven door to check a muffin with a toothpick. "Not quite done," she said. "That's the hard part about finding something good. Much easier to go along telling ourselves we don't need it."

"Are we talking about me or you?"

Claire smiled and lifted a shoulder. "Clayton is an interesting man."

"So you had a good time last night?"

"We did. Nice having a man on the other side of the dinner table. Nice, but not necessary."

"What do you mean?"

"Oh, just that for a long time, I felt like there must be something wrong with me. That your father's leaving the way he did proved that."

Addy dropped her gaze under a wave of guilt. "And I didn't help any."

Claire reached over and covered Addy's hand with hers. "You were trying to make sense of it the best you could."

"I put all the blame in the wrong place, though."

"Water under the bridge."

Addy looked up at her mother. "Thank you.

After everything I've been through with Mark, I'm not sure I could be as forgiving as you if I had a daughter who refused to see the truth."

Claire shook her head. "Sometimes the truth is just too painful, honey. And we need to filter it through our own interpretation so it's somehow manageable to us."

"The part I'm sorry about is how much it must have hurt you. Growing up, I was so sure I wanted to be something different from you. Now, I realize how lucky I would be to be half the woman you are."

Claire's eyes glistened with tears. "Oh, honey. Thank you. I'm just happy you're here. And that whatever happens, we've had this time together."

Addy nodded, reached out and hugged her mother, her throat tight. They sat that way for a good while, and she felt the forging of a new bond between them. One for which she was indescribably grateful.

Claire stood, rubbed a hand across Addy's hair, then went upstairs to get dressed. Addy sat at the table, drinking a second cup of coffee. She felt the terrible waste of all the years she had not allowed herself to see the similarities between her mother and herself. And the irony that they should end up in a nearly parallel place of decision. To stay on the path that was familiar and safe. Or find the courage to reach for the good.

She knew which one she thought her mother should do. And maybe in that, she'd found the answer to what she felt for Culley as well.

HE CALLED AROUND NOON. Addy had taken her cell phone out to the warehouse, asking Claire to give him the number if he called the house. She'd been working on the old office there all morning, cleaning it up, organizing files of invoices and customer information with the intent of setting it all up on computer for the future.

With the ringing of the phone, her heart kicked up a dozen beats. The sound of his voice sent it yet higher.

"Are you grounded?" he teased.

Addy smiled. "Mama had a pretty nice evening of her own. Took some of the focus off my indecent arrival home."

"Good. Would I be moving too fast if I asked you to dinner tonight?"

"No," she said, surprising herself with the certainty of her answer.

"Okay," he said, sounding pleased. "Pick you up at seven?"

"Seven would be great."

THE TAXI PULLED UP in front of the house just before six o'clock that evening. Liz pulled a ten out
of her purse, paid the driver, then got out and waited
while he retrieved her single suitcase from the trunk.

The driver got back in the taxi and drove off in
a puff of black exhaust. She stood there at the
edge of the paved driveway, transfixed by her own
uncertainty.

She'd taken a Greyhound bus from Mecklinburg, her stomach uneasy the entire way. Maybe
it wasn't right to just show up like this. Maybe she
should have called first.

Her hand trembled on the suitcase handle, and
she shuddered beneath the need for a drink.

After all this time, her mind still made that immediate leap to alcohol. The hold had not less-
ened. The only difference was that she could see
it for what it was, a dependence that lured with
knee-weakening appeal. So easy to give in to the
call of that one drink. To remember how it would
dull the reality of what she was about to do, take
the edge off her agony.

It would be so much easier to give in than stand
here in front of Culley's house with all her faults
and mistakes, trying to gather up the courage to
face her daughter.

She reached down for the suitcase, made her

way up the front steps, knocked on the door, then clenched her fist together to keep her fingers from shaking.

Footsteps sounded from inside, the door opened and there stood Madeline. Her daughter. Her throat immediately closed up, and she could not speak.

"Mama?"

"Hello, sweetheart."

Culley appeared behind her, a protective hand on Madeline's shoulder. "Liz. My God. What are you doing here?"

She swallowed hard, looking at Madeline. "I wanted to see you, honey. I know I should have called first."

Culley dropped a glance at Madeline who had gone pale with surprise. His face hardened. "Yes, you should have."

"I'm sorry. I just—"

"You're not in jail anymore?" Madeline asked.

Liz met her daughter's wary gaze and shook her head. "No."

"Are you going to stay here?"

Liz looked up at Culley, saw the anger in his eyes, could not blame him for it. "I just came to see you, honey."

Culley squeezed Madeline's shoulder, then

stepped back, as if forcing himself to think about her instead of his own feelings. That was the thing that had always set him apart from her as a parent. He had put their daughter first, and she had not.

"Come in, Liz," he said, taking her suitcase.

She released a sigh of relief and went inside.

ADDY WAS DRESSED and ready well before seven. Too early because now she had nothing to do but watch the clock in the living room tick forward, while she fought back an increasing wave of nerves. It was like being sixteen all over again, this nearly consuming need to see him.

At seven o'clock, she went outside and sat down on the porch step.

At seven-fifteen, she went back inside, opened her new laptop and tried to focus on an article she'd downloaded from the Internet.

By seven-thirty, she had no idea what she'd just read. She began to worry. It wasn't like Culley to be late. Or not to call.

Had he had second thoughts?

Stop! She was being ridiculous. The reasonable thing to do was call. Just call. Make sure everything was okay.

She went in the kitchen and picked up the phone, dialing the number. Madeline answered.

"Hi, it's Addy. I was wondering if your daddy had left yet."

"He's talking to Mama. She came home today."

Surprise hit Addy in the center of the chest. Liz was home? It took her a moment to let the information settle.

"Does this mean we can't go shopping anymore, Addy?"

"I don't know," she said, hearing what sounded like sadness in the child's voice. "I hope not."

"Me, too."

"Are you okay?"

There was silence for a moment, and then Madeline said, "Grown-ups are hard to understand sometimes."

"Everything will be all right," Addy said. "It's just not always easy to see that."

"I guess so."

"Okay. I should let you go. Talk to you soon?"

"Bye, Addy."

She stood there holding the phone long after the line had been disconnected. Then finally placed it back on the wall mount, went upstairs and changed clothes.

THE PHONE RANG at just after ten.

Addy was in bed with a book propped in front of her, a futile exercise in distraction. Claire wasn't home yet, so she reached for the extension beside her bed, certain it was Culley before she heard his voice.

"Hey."

"Hi."

"I'm not sure where to start."

"You don't have to."

"Yeah, I do."

"Culley—"

"Madeline said you called. So you know Liz is here?"

"Yeah."

"Addy, I had no idea—"

"You don't have to explain anything," she said in a soft voice. "It has nothing to do with me."

"It has everything to do with you," he said, the words losing ground to frustration. He paused, and then said, "I want so damn badly to be past all this."

"It doesn't work like that though, does it?"

"I thought I'd reached a point where I could go on, make another life."

"But she needs you."

Another pause. "She needs someone."

"And I know you. If you walk away from this before it's finished in a way you can live with, you'll regret it."

"So what are you saying?"

"Do what you need to do. Be who you are."

"I'm not sure I know who that is."

"I do. You're a man who stays where he's needed."

Several beats of silence. "And what about us?"

She chose her words. They did not come easily. "If what we have has a place, it can wait."

"Addy—"

"It's late. I should go."

"I'll call you."

"Okay," she said and hung up. She sat for a moment, then went into the bathroom and turned on the shower. She pulled her nightgown over her head and stepped under the warm spray, standing there until she couldn't be sure whether the moisture running down her face was water or tears.

CULLEY STOOD FOR a moment with his hand on the telephone, fighting the urge to call her back.

"I messed up your plans for the night, didn't I?"

He whirled around. Liz stood in the kitchen doorway, looking regretful. He sighed and said, "It's okay."

"It's not. I know it. You have another life now

which is perfectly understandable. I don't intend
to mess that up. I just want to spend some time
with Madeline."

He nodded.

She looked as though she wanted to say something else, then said, "I think I'll go up. I'm kind
of beat."

"Good night, Liz," he said.

"Good night."

FOR THE NEXT WEEK, Addy made every effort to
keep busy. She hired a full-time man to help with
the orchard. Then threw herself into writing a business plan, determined to iron the details out on paper
as proof that what she was proposing could work.

Claire was skeptical at first, but with each piece
of the plan Addy put in front of her, skepticism
began to turn to enthusiasm.

On Sunday, they were sitting at the kitchen
table, papers spread out in front of them. "I've put
together a list of equipment we can repair and
things we won't be able to avoid buying. I've also
made a list of interesting varieties I think we
should consider planting, specialty apples that
should go for a higher price to some of these gour-
met places who look for ways to be different—"

"Addy."

She looked up and found Claire studying her with a worried expression. "What is it?"

"You," she said. "You've been going from one thing to another all week as if there's a fire to put out. Want to talk about it?"

She shook her head. "There's nothing to talk about."

"I know Liz is back," Claire said.

Addy looked up, met her mother's compassionate gaze. The wall she'd built around herself this past week suddenly crumpled, and she put an elbow on the table, dropping her head onto one hand. "He's doing the right thing. It couldn't be any other way."

"For either of you," Claire agreed. "Sometimes, honey, it takes time for things to become what they're going to be. If you and Culley are meant to be, then this will all work out."

Addy knew she was right. Hard as the words were to hear.

CHAPTER SEVENTEEN

LATER THAT EVENING, Addy was at the barn feeding the deer when she heard a car pull in the driveway.

She stuck her head outside the door and saw Doc Nolen's old Jeep. He was standing at the foot of the porch steps talking to her mom. Claire was smiling at something he was saying, and it struck Addy how incredibly pretty she looked. Lit up in a way that made her look young and happy.

She ducked back inside the barn before they saw her. A few minutes later, the door opened, and the two of them came to the stall door.

Addy stood, brushing her hands on her jeans. "Hey, Doc."

"Addy. I just dropped by to see how our patient was doing."

The deer whirled and ran to the corner of the stall, turning to look back at them with wide, wary eyes.

"She's a little uneasy around anyone she doesn't know," Addy said.

"That's good, though," Doc said. "You don't want her to become too trusting. I see she hasn't lacked for food. She's plumped up quite a bit."

She smiled. "She likes to eat."

"Addy's taken really good care of her," Claire said. "I'm not so sure she's going to be able to let her go."

"Have you thought about that?" Doc asked.

Addy lifted her shoulders. "Not a lot."

"I'm guessing she's old enough to be released. August would be the latest to let her go, so she'll have enough time to learn how to forage before the winter."

The words left a pit in Addy's stomach. Of course, she had known the time would come when she would need to put the deer back where she belonged. She couldn't stay here in this stall forever. "Mama's right," she said. "It won't be easy."

"You did a good thing for her. She probably wouldn't have made it if you and Culley hadn't pulled her out of the woods."

"Thanks," Addy said.

"Well, I'd better get going." Doc looked at Claire and cleared his throat. "Word is there's a pretty good band playing out at the recreation park tonight. Some kind of pop country. I thought I might ride out there and have a listen. Any interest in going with me?"

Claire shook her head. "Oh, I can't. I'm not dressed or—"

"You look just right," he said.

"You do, Mama," Addy said. "Go."

Claire hesitated and then, "Well, why not? That does sound like fun, Clayton. Just let me get my purse."

Addy walked outside with them, waved a few minutes later when they headed down the driveway. Maybe it would work out between them. If it was meant to be. She really hoped that it was.

ON MONDAY MORNING, just over a week since Liz's return, Culley sat in his office, hands around a mug of untouched coffee. He felt as if he were moving on automatic pilot, as if overnight his life had turned into one he didn't recognize.

He had to give Liz credit for her effort with Madeline. She took her for walks, baked cookies, went to movies, all things she'd never done before as a mother because her addiction had been her preoccupation.

But so far Madeline wasn't lowering the wall she'd erected around her feelings for her mother.

She rarely smiled, took part in the activities Liz suggested with obvious reluctance.

Culley actually felt sorry for Liz. He could see how desperately she craved her daughter's forgiveness, but Madeline's relationship with her mother was one she would have to define herself. It wasn't up to him.

The only thing he could do was allow the two of them time. And he was torn between the desire to do the right thing and his own need to see Addy.

He stared at the phone, reached for the receiver, dialed the first three digits, then stopped. He placed it back in the cradle. He had nothing to offer her right now.

Addy was right. He wasn't free and clear. She deserved nothing less than that.

He got up and started his day.

ON MONDAY MORNING, Ellen called.

Addy was at her laptop, putting together a promotional flyer to send to potential customers. She sat back in her chair, glad to hear her friend's voice.

They updated each other on things, and then Ellen said, "And Culley? How's that going?"

"It's not at the moment," Addy said.

"What happened?"

"Nothing I want to go into right now."

"So maybe I called at the right time."

"What is it?"

"The partners held a meeting on Friday and called me in first thing this morning. They're hooking up with Burkley, Lane in New York. They want to place two top-notch corporate attorneys in their office who will do things the way they like them done. They picked me. And they want you to reconsider your resignation."

"What?"

"Yep. You interested?"

"I don't know. You caught me by surprise."

"I know you're helping your mom out, but I have to say this is a great opportunity. Can you come up and talk?"

"Could I think about it?"

"Sure. But they want to know soon. Can you call me tomorrow?"

"I will."

"Talk to you then."

Addy hung up and sat for a moment, thinking.

Claire walked into the room and set a cup of tea on the desk. "I thought you might like some."

"Thank you," Addy said.

"Are you all right?"

"Just a little surprised. That was Ellen. My

friend from work. My old firm has joined ranks with a New York firm and wants to place two attorneys in the Manhattan office right away. They've asked Ellen and me to consider the positions."

Claire's smile faltered a bit, then steadied. "It sounds like a great opportunity, honey."

"They want me to come up and talk up about it."

"Are you going?"

"There's so much more to do here—"

"Go hear them out, at least. Then make your decision."

"But—"

"I don't want you to look back at some point and wish you'd done something differently."

Addy looked out the window, thought about Culley and how she'd said practically the same thing to him. The past week had not been an easy one. Being in the same place and not seeing him…she didn't imagine it would get any easier. "What about everything here?"

"You've already done the most important part. Finding a way to breathe new life into this place. If you decide you want to be a part of it, that will be wonderful. But I want you to make sure you know what you're leaving behind. Then decide."

ADDY WENT TO the barn early the next morning. During the short time she'd slept, her dreams had been a tangle of scenes in which she tried to let the deer go, but Culley kept standing in the way, imploring her not to.

She'd sat straight up in bed, her face wet with sweat as if she'd just run five miles. She'd sat there a moment, knowing what she had to do.

It wasn't yet six when she let herself into the stall. The deer was still asleep, but at Addy's entrance, raised her head.

"Hey, sleepy girl," she said, rubbing her soft neck.

The deer licked her hand. Addy pulled some carrots out of her pocket, the mini kind the deer liked best and fed them to her. She followed that up with some apple slices. "You're going to be okay, you know?"

The deer licked her hand again, nudged it in search of more treats. Addy removed a bottle of nail polish from her other pocket, uncapped it and made a bright red circle on the deer's right hip. She stood, then swiped a sudden release of tears from her cheeks. She was doing the right thing.

She opened the stall door and stood just outside holding it open. The deer looked at her, then trotted out and stood beside her. Addy walked away from the barn, the deer staying close to her side. When they'd reached the pond, she stopped, dropping down onto her knees. A field lay between them and the woods on the other side. She knew that a group of deer came down every morning for a drink.

They sat there for a few minutes, Addy rubbing her side. And then four deer appeared at the edge of the woods, walked across the field to the pond.

The deer looked at Addy, then bounded off, stopping short of the group. They had just spotted her.

Addy stood. The group turned and ran back to the woods. The little deer stared at her as if torn.

"Go," she said, raising her hand.

A fallen tree lay at the edge of the field that bordered the woods. She jumped it in a single leap and was gone after the others.

Addy cried.

She couldn't help it.

THAT AFTERNOON, CLAIRE received a call saying there would be a six o'clock meeting about the interstate route that evening at the community center.

Addy and Claire arrived to a nearly full room. They managed to find two chairs together near the back. A news team from a nearby TV affiliate stood near the front with cameras. A reporter from the Roanoke newspaper sat in the second row.

Mayor Duncan stood behind a podium at the front of the room. He raised a hand. "Could I have your attention, please, ladies and gentlemen? I won't hold you in suspense. This afternoon, we received a statement from Congressman Powers's office indicating that he no longer supports the proposal of Corridor A for Interstate 92. The statement read as follows. 'Recent cost estimates have revealed Corridor B, the route that falls to the west side of the county, around Three Hawk mountain, would involve the fewest disturbances of existing businesses and home sites while providing a direct path for the transportation demands that must be met.'" The mayor looked up from the paper and smiled a big smile.

Addy reached for Claire's hand and gave it a squeeze. Claire squeezed back.

"In conclusion, I understand that tomorrow's paper will begin a series of articles looking at the connection between Congressman Powers and one of his most prominent supporters, Raymond Dudley. As you know, Mr. Dudley is under investigation for the threats that were made against many of you in relation to the willing sale of your property with regard to the Harper's Mill route. I look forward to reading those articles."

Everyone stood and started clapping. Addy embraced her mother, aware of the relief on her face. The mood turned festive then, hugs and backslapping all around.

The meeting was adjourned. Claire spotted a friend from church with whom she wanted to speak.

"I'll meet you by the car," Addy said.

"I'll just be a minute."

Addy made her way to the stairs, coming up short at the sight of Culley waiting at the bottom.

"Hey," she said.

"Hey. Walk you out?"

"Sure," she said, her heart doing an uncooperative leap.

Outside, they stopped at her car. Stood in a clutch of awkwardness as if neither knew what to say to the other.

"Good news," he said.

"It is. It'll be interesting to see the article tomorrow."

"My friend at the paper gave me an advance reading. It looks like Congressman Powers had some major incentive from Dudley to make sure the road went through Harper's Mill."

"Financial incentive?"

"Kickbacks on the contracts Dudley stood to gain, which apparently amounted to a good deal of money."

"I guess that's one way to increase your retirement fund."

"Yeah," he said, his gaze direct on hers. "I'm just glad they didn't get away with it."

"And that no one else has to worry about being the next target."

He nodded. "You look great, Addy."

"Thanks."

"Are you all right?" he asked, his voice softening a note.

"I'm okay," she said.

"I miss you."

"Culley—"

"I know," he said, holding up a hand. "Nowhere to go. I just wanted you to know."

She glanced down, then looked back up at him. "I got a call today about a job offer."

Surprise flickered across his face. "A job?"

"In Manhattan. My old firm is merging with a firm there."

"Oh." Long pause. "And you're interested?"

She lifted both shoulders. "I don't know. Mama thinks I need to consider it. Make sure I know what I'm turning down."

He started to say something, stopped. Then nodded once. "She's right."

It wasn't what she'd expected him to say. So why had she told him anyway? Had she hoped he would plead with her not to go?

Claire came out. "Hello, Culley."

He cleared his throat. "How are you, Claire?"

"Good. You?"

"Fine, thanks."

"I can go back in for a bit if you two would like to talk."

"No," Addy said, suddenly needing to put some space between Culley and the pain in her heart. "We should go, Mama."

He nodded and stepped back.

"Bye," Addy said.

"Bye."

She pulled away from the curb, glancing once in the rearview mirror. He was still standing there, hands in his pockets, watching them go.

CHAPTER EIGHTEEN

CLEMENTS OCCUPIED AN old train depot on the out-
skirts of town. Culley drove by it every day, normally not giving it a glance. But tonight was
different. Tonight, it pulled at him with an insist-
ence he could not refuse. For the first time in
longer than he could remember, he felt the need
for a drink.

He wheeled into the parking lot and got out,
heading inside where he blinked for a moment
to adjust to the dim lighting. He took a seat at
the bar.

The bartender was John Wayne-tall with a voice
to match. "What can I get you?" he asked.

"Scotch and water, please."

The bartender nodded, reached for a bottle,
poured a measure in a short glass, added some
water and handed it to him on a napkin.

Culley put his elbows on the bar, stared down
at the drink.

"Rough day?"

To his right sat a man in bib overalls and a worn-looking plaid shirt. Culley tipped his head. "Yeah. Sort of."

"You're looking at that glass like it's no friend."

"I guess it isn't."

The man took a sip of his beer. "I don't have to tell you there aren't any answers in the bottom. Not much peace, either."

Culley rubbed his thumb around the rim of the scotch and water.

"You're Dr. Rutherford, aren't you?"

"Yeah."

The man stuck out his hand. "Barry Miller. My mother is one of your patients."

Culley shook his hand. "Evelyn Miller?"

Barry nodded.

"Nice woman, your mother."

"Thank you."

They sat a bit, not saying anything.

"You don't strike me as the kind of guy to come to a place like this for answers."

"I wouldn't, ordinarily."

"That big a problem, huh?"

"Pretty big."

"Woman troubles?"

"So to speak."

"You love her?"

It wasn't where Culley would have imagined ending up tonight, sitting on a stool in Clements discussing his personal life with a man he didn't know. But there was something about his manner that said he wasn't asking out of idle curiosity, so Culley answered. "Yes."

"Have you told her?"

Culley shook his head.

"Why's that?"

"I'm not exactly free and clear."

"You're married?"

"No. But my ex-wife is…she's kind of going through a rough time."

"And you're trying to fix it for her?"

"Trying to help, I guess."

"I don't have anything close to a degree in psychology, but I know a little something about trying to be all things to all people. That sometimes it makes us not much good to anyone."

Culley looked up, met the man's kind gaze. Nodded once. He pushed the glass to the edge of the bar and stood. "Thanks."

"I didn't tell you anything you didn't already know."

"Maybe I just needed to hear it."

LIZ WAS DOWNSTAIRS in the living room when Culley arrived home. He stopped in the doorway. She looked up and smiled.

"Madeline's not back yet?"

Liz got up from the couch, placed the magazine she'd been looking at on the coffee table. "Your mom said the church dinner would be over around eight-thirty."

Awkwardness settled over them. Culley nodded and said, "I have some calls to make."

"Okay."

He turned to go just as she called out, "Culley, wait."

"What is it?"

She crossed the living room floor, waving a hand between them. "Us," she said. "This silence between us. Are you going to punish me forever?"

Culley planted a hand on the doorjamb as if he needed the support to remain where he stood. "I'm not punishing you, Liz."

"It feels like you are," she said.

He noticed then the extra effort she'd taken with her appearance. Her hair was freshly washed and shiny. She'd put on makeup for the first time since she'd been back. And he could smell the subtle lift of perfume.

He drew in a deep breath and released it. "I want to be fair to you," he said.

"You've been more than fair to me." She looked down, then directly in his eyes. "I guess maybe on some level I hoped we might be more than that again."

Culley chose his words carefully. "I don't want to hurt you. But it can't be like that."

She reached out and placed a hand on his chest. "We had something really good once, didn't we?"

"Liz—"

She leaned in then and kissed him, her arms slipping around his neck. He let it go for a moment, then put his hands on her shoulders and stepped back.

Hurt flashed across her face—it was impossible to miss.

"I'm sorry," he said.

"You won't ever get past what I did, will you?"

"It's not that."

"Then what is it?"

He looked away.

"There's someone else?" she asked.

He glanced back, met her eyes. "Yes," he said. "There is."

She nodded, bit her lip, then forced a smile. "I see. Then I'm the one who should apologize."

"Liz—"

She held up a hand. "I've been an idiot, thinking I could ever make up for the past."

"No one's asking you to. We just need to figure out how to go on from here."

She forced a smile. "That's the trick, huh? I think I'll go on up. Good night, Culley."

"Liz—"

But she didn't stop. And he let her go.

ADDY LEFT THE HOUSE around five-thirty and arrived in D.C. just before ten with a break in Staunton for a quick breakfast at Rowe's, a must-stop when traveling I-81.

Owings, Blake occupied the seventh floor of a high-end office building in the heart of D.C. When Addy had first come to work there eight years ago, she'd been impressed with all the bells and whistles that go with a prestigious law firm. A waiting room straight out of *Architectural Digest* with enormous black leather sofas and original art work on the faux-painted walls. But as she stood at the front desk now waiting for the new receptionist she didn't know to buzz Ellen, she felt a quick longing for the sound of a tractor and an apple-scented breeze.

"Ellen said to send you right back, Ms. Taylor," the receptionist said.

"Thank you." Addy followed the hall to Ellen's office, knocked at the half-closed door.

"That you, Addy?"

Addy stuck her head around the corner. Ellen vaulted out of her chair, wrapped her in a big hug, then pulled back for an assessment. "I can't argue that life away from the big city has been good for you."

"Thanks. You look amazing, as always."

"Want some coffee or something?"

"No. I'm good, thanks."

"So what do you think? Are you up for a move to Manhattan?"

"I thought I should hear out the offer."

"Fair enough. What's holding you back?"

"It's kind of complicated."

"Involving the infamous Culley?"

Addy tipped her head to one side, avoiding the question.

"Complicated how?"

"I'm not the only one in the picture," she said, not wanting to elaborate beyond that. On the drive up, she'd thought of little else, and the more she went over it, the more hopeless it seemed.

"Ah." Ellen bit her lip in characteristic consideration. "So maybe some distance would be best.

And if what you two have is the real thing, it'll find a way."

Addy knew it was true. That maybe this wasn't their time. That the last thing she wanted was for Culley to wake up one day and regret something he hadn't done because of her. And maybe it would be easier for him if she weren't in Harper's Mill.

"Besides," Ellen said. "Can you imagine how much fun we could have in Manhattan?"

"And you've already mapped out the hot spots, right?"

"Of course." Ellen smiled. "Roland's waiting in his office. Shall we go?"

"After you," Addy said.

THE ITCH WAS SO strong she could barely think around it.

Liz stood at the kitchen window, arms locked across her chest as if she could physically hold herself together, when inside, she felt the pieces flying apart.

She wanted to be strong. Craved it almost as much as the alcohol. Almost.

What she really wanted was oblivion. From the mistakes she'd made. From the reserve she saw in her daughter's eyes every time she looked at her. From the tolerance and sympathy in Culley's.

What had she been thinking? Had she really believed she could come back and expect everyone to start over? Pretend nothing had happened?

From where she was standing now, it seemed incredibly naive.

She glanced at her watch. Ten in the morning, and she had nothing to do until Madeline got home from school. Six hours. No, eight, because Ida was taking her to ballet at four. Eight hours.

She went to the freezer, pulled out a bag of coffee beans, put some in the grinder and made a strong pot. She sat at the kitchen table and drank three cups, one after the other as if the caffeine might soften the itch.

She cleaned up the dishes from breakfast, put them away in the cupboards. Ten-forty.

She ran a hand through her hair, catching a glimpse of herself in the mirror hanging on the far wall. Saw the reflection of a woman losing the battle.

She went to the coat closet and pulled out her purse. She walked out on the porch, stood for a few moments, looking down the road.

She had no car. So she started walking.

CULLEY LEFT THE OFFICE just before six. His mom had called to say her car wouldn't start, so he headed over to the dance studio to pick up Madeline from ballet class.

She was waiting for him at the door, climbing into the Explorer with a big smile on her face. She rattled off all the details of the class and the upcoming recital to which she would wear her new dress.

They were almost home when Culley's cell phone rang. He picked it up—his office number was on caller ID.

"Hey, Culley. It's Tracy. I wasn't sure what to do with this, but someone just called from Clements. They said Liz had been there since early afternoon. They wanted to know if someone could come and get her."

Culley dropped his head back against the seat. "Ah, could you call them back and tell them I'll be there just as soon as I run Madeline over to Mom's?"

"They said within ten minutes, or they'd have to call the police," she said, apology in her voice.

"Thanks, Tracy," Culley said, clicking off the phone.

"Is it Mama?" Madeline looked at him with resignation in her eyes.

"We need to go pick her up," he said.

Madeline nodded once, then turned and looked out the window.

A BOUNCER STOOD at the front door of Clements, apparently acting as a barricade to prevent Liz from coming back in. She sat on the top step of the entrance, elbows on her knees, hands pushed up through her hair.

"Is she okay, Daddy?"

Culley squeezed her hand and said, "I'll be right back."

He got out and jogged over to the entrance, stopping just short of the steps.

The bouncer inclined his head. "You here to pick her up?"

"Yeah," Culley said.

"Probably looks like she was overserved, but she'd had a few before she got here."

"Thanks."

The bouncer turned and went back inside.

Liz looked up at him and shook her head.

"Can you walk?" he asked.

She tried to stand but couldn't manage it.

Culley bent down and picked her up, carried her to the Explorer and set her in the back seat. The smell of vomit was strong on her clothes. He went around back, found a plastic bowl he kept in the car for Madeline's occasional motion sickness. He handed it to Liz. "Are you okay?"

She nodded, hands hiding her face.

Culley got in the driver's side and started the vehicle. He pulled out of the parking lot onto the main road, glancing at Madeline who was sitting ramrod straight in her seat, a single tear sliding down her face.

And with that, he wasn't sure what he felt more: fury or despair.

As soon as he got home, Culley carried Liz upstairs and set her in the shower, clothes and all. He went into the bedroom and dialed Addy's number. Claire answered the phone.

"Hey, Claire. Is Addy there?"

"No. She went up to D.C. for that job interview."

What felt like a physical pain slammed through his chest.

"Is something wrong?"

He sighed. "Yeah. Actually, there is. Do you think you could come get Madeline and let her spend the night with you? Mom's car isn't working, and—"

"Say no more. I'll be there in a few minutes."

"Thank you, Claire." He hung up, her words reverberating in his head like beads in a can, the rattle so loud he couldn't focus. But he couldn't think about Addy right now or what any of that might mean. Right now, he had to take care of Liz.

CLAIRE HAD COME to the door just before seven-thirty, putting her arm around Madeline and guiding her out to her car, Hershey at their heels. Culley had watched them go with a weight on his heart, wishing he could have spared his daughter what she had seen. If he'd had any idea what kind of shape Liz was in, he would never have taken her.

Liz sat under the cold spray of the shower for over a half hour. He sat outside on the floor, waiting for the alcohol to loosen its hold. She finally stood, and he helped her out.

"Can you get out of those clothes?"

She nodded.

"I'll go make some coffee," he said.

"Culley?" she called out just as he was closing the door.

"Yeah?"

"I'm sorry."

He stared at her for a moment, then turned and walked out. He'd heard it all before.

A LITTLE WHILE LATER, he took the coffee up and left it on her nightstand. She was in bed, one arm thrown over her face. She said nothing, and he left, not trusting himself to speak.

He was in his office doing paperwork when he heard her come down the stairs. It was after ten, and he had expected her to sleep it off through the night.

She stood in the doorway, meeting his gaze with what looked like paper-thin courage. "Can we talk?" she asked.

He pushed back from his desk. "Is there anything to say?"

She came into the room, sat in the chair across from him, eyes on her folded hands. She looked up and said, "Probably nothing that would mean anything."

"Why, Liz? Why?"

She lifted both shoulders, tears running down her cheeks. She swiped them away and said, "I wish I knew."

"My God, Liz, do you have any idea what this did to Madeline?"

"I know." The words were little more than a whisper. "I know."

They sat in silence for a long time, until finally, she spoke again. "When I came here, I had convinced myself I was doing so with the intention of standing on my own two feet. But I realize now I did what I've always done. Came running back to you, hoping you could fix it. Make everything better."

"Liz—"

"No. Please. Let me finish." She looked down for a few moments, then raised her eyes to his. "I think sometimes we look for people who by their own kindness help prop us up. Keep us from seeing ourselves as we really are. I know you've wanted to help me, Culley. Too many times to count. I've hung this chain of guilt around your neck. And I was willing to pretend that was okay because it meant I could stay here and do the same thing I did before. Look to you for the answers. But it's time I found the answers in myself."

"I do want to help you, Liz."

"Then can you find someplace to take me tonight?"

"It can wait until morning. You don't have to do this tonight."

"I want to. If I wait, I'll change my mind." She stood, pressing her palms against the front of her jeans. "I'm going upstairs to pack my things and call my probation officer."

"Are you sure?"

"I'm sure," she said.

THEY DROVE THE four hours to Alexandria, arriving at the rehab center in the middle of the night. Culley went inside with Liz, standing to the side while she admitted herself.

A nurse came out and took Liz's single suitcase. "Ready when you are," she said.

Liz turned to Culley. "I'm going to get it right this time. I want you to do the same."

"You'll be okay?"

She pressed her lips together and nodded. "Tell Madeline I'm sorry."

"Just get better, okay. That's all she'll need to hear." He put an arm around her neck, hugged her to him.

She leaned into him for a moment, then stepped back and looked at the nurse. "Okay. I'm ready."

"This way then," the nurse said kindly, waving a hand at a set of double doors.

"Liz?"

She glanced back.

"Call, okay?"

"I will." She stepped through the double doors and was gone.

ADDY LEFT D.C. early on Thursday morning, anxious to get home. It was nearly eleven when she turned onto the orchard road. Apple trees heavy with fruit appeared on the right side of the car, and she was filled with a sudden gladness to see them.

Halfway up the gravel road, she spotted a car in her rearview mirror. Culley's Explorer. Her heart jumped a beat.

He followed her to the house and pulled into the driveway beside her. She got out, extraordinarily glad to see him. But the look on his face made her smile fade.

"Hi," she said.

"Hi."

"Are you okay?"

"Yeah. Or will be. I just came to pick up Madeline. She stayed with your mom last night."

Just then Madeline came running out of the house, straight into Culley's arms. He locked her in a hug, pressed his face to her neck. "Hey, little bean. You okay?"

She nodded, then pulled back to look at him with a solemn face. "Is Mama all right?"

"I think she's going to be."

Claire came out, a dish towel in her hands, Hershey behind her. "Hi, honey," she said to Addy. "How was your trip?"

"Good," Addy said.

"I think I'll just keep her, Culley," Claire said, a hand on Madeline's hair. "She's a good little helper. And Hershey's been good for Peabody. He's still recovering from the shock."

Madeline smiled.

"Thank you, Claire. I really appreciate it. I guess we better be going."

"Culley," Addy said, "can we talk for a minute?"

He met her gaze, and then, "Yeah."

"Madeline, let's go finish making those cookies," Claire said. "Then we'll pack up a tin for you to take home with you."

Madeline slid out of Culley's arms, took Claire's hand and followed her back in the house.

Once it was just the two of them, Addy felt awkward. "Walk out to the pond?"

"Sure," he said.

They walked down to the gate at the end of the yard, opened it and headed across the field they had walked so many times before. The morning was giving way to afternoon, the sun high in a crisp blue sky. They stepped onto the old dock at the edge of the pond, the boards creaking beneath their feet.

They stopped at the end, stood looking out at the water. Addy sat down. Culley sat beside her, a few inches of space between them.

"Are you all right?" she asked.

"I'm okay," he said, shoving his hands in the

pockets of faded blue jeans. "Liz kind of had a relapse last night. Someone from Clements called me to come and get her."

"Is she—"

"She's fine. It was pretty awful. After it was all over, she asked me to take her to a treatment center in Alexandria. I just got back this morning."

"Oh, Culley. I'm sorry."

He shook his head. "I think she may just be okay this time. There was something different in her last night. A resolve I've never heard before."

"I hope so."

"I realized something yesterday, too."

"What?"

He looked down at the water. "That I've been a crutch for her. I'm not sure if it was for her or for my own sense of helping her like I could never help my dad. But I can't do that anymore."

"You were trying to do the right thing," Addy said, turning her head to look at him. "I know that."

He lifted a shoulder. "Yeah, good intentions."

She put a hand on his arm. "You can't blame yourself."

He dropped his head back to look up at the sky. "I don't. A long time ago, I did. But it's just a pretty horrible thing to see a person go through."

They sat there for a few minutes, not talking.

Addy sensed it was what he needed, and she wanted, more than anything, just to be there for him.

Two ducks swooped in and landed in the center of the pond. They swam in a circle, the female lifting her feathers, then pecking at the surface of the water for food.

"So. You're taking the job?" Culley's gaze was set on the ducks, his voice neutral.

Addy reached a hand into the water, letting it slide through her fingers. "No."

He looked at her, surprise in his eyes. "But I thought—"

She shook her head. "Maybe I needed to prove to myself that I was making the right choice to stay here. It was a good offer. A great offer. My friend Ellen thinks I'm crazy, but I just…nothing about it felt right. I walked in that office, listened to what the senior partner had to say and I knew without a doubt that I wanted to be here."

"Yeah?"

She looked up at the sky. "I guess I've realized that maybe the not-so-great things that happen to us—in my case, Mark's affair—are a chance to look at where we're going, decide whether or not we've been headed in the right direction. I don't regret my work in D.C., but I'd like to make a go of this orchard. And maybe down the road, open a practice here in town."

Culley looked at her, smiled a half smile that had relief at its edges. "That sounds really great."

"You think?" she asked, looking at him now.

"I do," he said.

They held each other's gaze for a few moments. He leaned in and brushed her mouth with his. She kissed him back, and there under the warm noon sun, they took their time with it. Reuniting.

He put a hand to the back of her neck and brushed her jaw with his thumb. "I really missed you," he said.

"I missed you, too."

"So what about us? Can this work?"

On the other side of the pond, a small deer appeared. Behind her were two other deer. The smaller deer stared at them for a moment, then walked down to the water to take a long drink.

Addy put a hand to her chest, her breath suspended there.

The deer turned and walked back to the other two. On her right hip was the small circle of red nail polish Addy had painted on before setting her free.

She looked at Culley and smiled. "Yeah. I think it can."

Claire Taylor's Virginia Apple Pie

Six Red Delicious apples, thinly sliced with peel
1 1/2 cups old-fashioned oatmeal
1 cup brown sugar
1/2 cup whole wheat flour
3/4 cup melted butter
Butter 9" glass pie plate. Place sliced apples on
bottom. Mix together flour, sugar and oatmeal.
Spread over apples. Drizzle melted butter over
top. Bake at 350° for 30 minutes or so.

Easy and delicious!

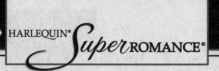

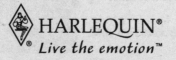

Street Smart
TARA TAYLOR QUINN

Escape and illusions...

Francesca Witting has
come to Las Vegas in
search of her runaway
half sister, Autumn Stevens.
There she meets Luke Everson,
an ex-marine and head of
security, who intends to start
a family by adopting a child
without the "claustrophobia"
of marriage.

**Connections and
dreaming big...**

But when Francesca discovers
an unknown connection between
Autumn and Luke, she must
decide if finding love with Luke
is the biggest dream of all.

**"Quinn writes touching
stories about real people
that transcend plot type
or genre."**
**—Rachel Potter,
*All About Romance***

*Available in July 2004,
wherever books are sold.*

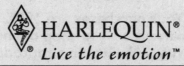

If you enjoyed what you just read,
then we've got an offer you can't resist!

Take 2 bestselling
love stories FREE!
Plus get a FREE surprise gift!

Clip this page and mail it to Harlequin Reader Service®

IN U.S.A.	IN CANADA
3010 Walden Ave.	P.O. Box 609
P.O. Box 1867	Fort Erie, Ontario
Buffalo, N.Y. 14240-1867	L2A 5X3

YES! Please send me 2 free Harlequin Superromance® novels and my free
surprise gift. After receiving them, if I don't wish to receive anymore, I can
return the shipping statement marked cancel. If I don't cancel, I will receive 6
brand-new novels every month, before they're available in stores. In the U.S.A.,
bill me at the bargain price of $4.69 plus 25¢ shipping and handling per book
and applicable sales tax, if any*. In Canada, bill me at the bargain price of $5.24
plus 25¢ shipping and handling per book and applicable taxes**. That's the
complete price, and a savings of at least 10% off the cover prices—what a
great deal! I understand that accepting the 2 free books and gift places me
under no obligation ever to buy any books. I can always return a shipment and
cancel at any time. Even if I never buy another book from Harlequin, the 2 free
books and gift are mine to keep forever.

135 HDN DZ7W
336 HDN DZ7X

Name	(PLEASE PRINT)	
Address	Apt.#	
City	State/Prov.	Zip/Postal Code

* Terms and prices subject to change without notice. Sales tax applicable in N.Y.
** Canadian residents will be charged applicable provincial taxes and GST.
   All orders subject to approval. Offer limited to one per household and not valid to
   current Harlequin Superromance® subscribers.
   ® are registered trademarks owned and used by the trademark owner and its licensee.

SUP04   ©2004 Harlequin Enterprises Limited

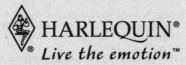

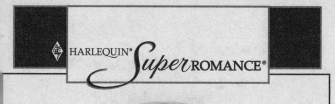

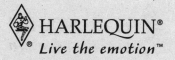

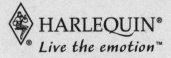